W9-BKE-496

THE MISSING MAP
OF PIRATE'S
HAVEN

The Accidental

DETECTIVES

THE MISSING MAP OF PIRATE'S HAVEN

SIGMUND BROUWER

VICTOR BOOKS®

A DIVISION OF SCRIPTURE PRESS PUBLICATIONS INC.
USA CANADA ENGLAND

THE ACCIDENTAL DETECTIVES SERIES
Lost Beneath Manhattan
The Mystery Tribe of Camp Blackeagle
Phantom Outlaw at Wolf Creek
The Disappearing Jewel of Madagascar
The Missing Map of Pirate's Haven
Creature of the Mists

Cover illustration by Suzanne Garnier
Photo by Dwight Arthur

Library of Congress Cataloging-in-Publication Data

Brouwer, Sigmund, 1959-
    The missing map of Pirate's Haven / Sigmund Brouwer.
        p.   cm. — (The Accidental detectives series ; 7)
    Summary: Twelve-year-old Ricky and his friends believe the secret of a
long-lost pirate treasure may be found through their summer job of re-
painting an old California house, whose owner's strange nocturnal activities and loss of faith in God present them with additional challenges.
    ISBN: 0-89693-858-1
    [1. Buried treasure — Fiction. 2. California — Fiction.
3. Christian life — Fiction. 4. Mystery and detective stories.]
I. Title. II. Series: Brouwer, Sigmund, 1959- Accidental
detectives : 7. PZ7.B79984Mil   1991   90-49844
[Fic] — dc20   CIP
                                            AC

©1991 by Sigmund Brouwer. All rights reserved.
Printed in the United States of America.

1 2 3 4 5 6 7 8 9 10 Printing/Year 95 94 93 92 91

VICTOR BOOKS
A division of SP Publications, Inc.
Wheaton, Illinois 60187

For the Davidsons:
Wayne, Karen, Courtney, and Chelsea

This is what you do with a kid brother who drives you nuts most of the time and then specifically drives you nuts by catching the biggest bass ever taken out of the Jamesville River. You get him to fish in a mud puddle.

The idea hit me at roughly 10:04 A.M. that summer morning as the three of us—Mike Andrews, Ralphy Zee, and me, Ricky Kidd—watched along the bank while my six-year-old brother Joel struggled to carry the bass with both hands. Its tail fin hung low enough to rub the top of his sneakers.

"I can't believe it," Mike muttered with disgust as he kicked a rock into the slow moving water of the Jamesville River. "I just can't believe it."

Mike was the one who had laughed at Joel's toy fishing rod.

Ralphy replayed the catch with admiration in his voice. "First of all, the kid manages to track us down to our secret spot. Even with our fancy dodge out the back of Jim's Pizza House. Scares Ricky into losing the only fish he's had in two days. Borrows the half-drowned worm Mike had used for half an hour. Then, wham! Hooks a monster and fights it for fifteen minutes without saying a word. And just when it's about to slip away, the kid wades in and grabs the monster by the gills. What a fish! I'll say it again." Ralphy whistled. "What a fi—"

"Spare us, OK?" Mike kicked another rock into the river. "We're a miserable bunch of twelve-year-olds to let ourselves be outfished by someone his size."

Joel worked his way up the grassy bank to where he had left his teddy bear.

Up to that point, I hadn't said a word. I was still trying to recover from the tap on my shoulder that had nearly sent me vaulting into the river. But then Joel usually does that to me.

He's like a personal ghost, the way he follows me everywhere. It seems he can get through locked doors and closed windows. Joel never says much when you do manage to spot him. Just stares and watches. He disappears as soon as you turn your head, and then reappears when you least expect it. Which is mostly when you're doing something you shouldn't. Those are the times I faint or have heart attacks or fall into disaster.

All I could say was, "See if he manages to do this to us in San Diego."

Mike grinned. "That's right, pal. Only one day left and then Southern California and sunny beaches. And no Joel. He can fish here every day for all I care."

That's the moment the idea hit me. "Maybe," I whispered slowly, "just maybe there's a way we can convince him to fish somewhere else."

Joel, above us on the bank, was showing the fish to his bear.

I turned to Ralphy. "How much money do you have on you?"

* * * * * * * *

Half an hour later, after his detour to the grocery store, Ralphy met us in downtown Jamesville on the Memorial Park bridge. Mike and I still carried all our fishing gear. A small creek ran beneath us on its way to the river. The park around the bridge was mainly scattered benches, clumps of small trees, and short groomed grass overlooked by City Hall and the town library. More important, for us anyway, was the tiny pond almost within the shadows of City Hall.

"Ralphy," Mike hissed, "Joel could be watching as we speak. Hide the bag!"

"But it stinks."

"So does leaving our secret fishing spot in that little twerp's hands. You want him to empty the entire river of bass while we're gone?"

Ralphy shoved the bag under his shirt.

We sauntered the last fifty yards to the pond. I had no doubt that Joel—teddy bear, huge bass, and toy fishing rod included— had managed to follow us this far.

Now came the tricky part.

"OK, Ralphy, bend over and drop the bag at the edge of the pond," I said quietly. "We can't allow Joel to see this."

As Ralphy slid the bag from his shirt, I surveyed the pond with satisfaction. *Perfect,* I told myself. *It's a glorified mud puddle.*

The pond was murky black, about the size of a basketball court, with a tired, mildewed marble mermaid water fountain that dribbled day and night. Green scum caked the pond's edges.

Within seconds, Mike and Ralphy were ready.

"Will it sink?" I asked.

Ralphy studied it carefully. "I think so. After all, the density of its mass must be greater than that of water and accordingly—"

"Knock it off, Einstein," Mike said. "It's big and frozen. Not warm and bloated. And I just jammed some rocks inside the belly. Don't worry, Ricky, it'll sink."

With that, Mike threw the frozen halibut into the center of the pond. One quick splash and it was gone.

Ralphy stared, almost mournfully, at the nylon line that ran from the fast-sinking halibut to the tip of Mike's fishing rod. "Sixteen bucks that fish cost us—five dollars and thirty-three-and-a-third cents apiece. I hope it's worth it."

"That depends—" I grinned—"on the kind of fight it gives Mike."

"Shhhh!" Mike nodded his head at a shadow approaching from behind me. By the time Joel arrived, Ralphy and I also had our lines in the water.

For once, I was ready for Joel's deathly quiet tap on the back of my shoulder. But when it came, I still jumped and landed with my ribs clutched in panic. After all, Joel needed to believe this was a normal situation.

"Maybe catch more fish," he said proudly, ignoring, as usual, any terror he might have caused.

To follow us, he had tied his precious teddy bear to the end of his fishing rod and carried that with his left hand. In his right hand, he held a thick forked stick that leaned back against his shoulder like a parade soldier's rifle. At the top of the stick, and hanging down Joel's back from the fork, was his large bass, hoisted through the gills.

We watched in fascination as he unloaded himself. First the stick, which he jabbed into the soft ground at the edge of the pond. The bass hung there in the cool morning air, making the three of us itch with envy.

Then, gently, Joel untied his teddy bear from the fishing line. He set it on the grass. Finally, he reached into his pocket and dug out the remains of the worm he had borrowed from Mike to catch the bass. He squinted to get it on the hook, then flipped his hook and line into the pond and sighed happily.

"Swim to them fish, worm," he said shyly to the water.

Joel doesn't say much. Not because he doesn't know the words. He can read better than most kids his age. But he mispronounces words once in a while so he says as little as possible. And by nature he's quiet anyway. Most ghosts are.

I wanted to tell Joel right then that worms don't swim, especially squished ones, but he had the bass heavy beside him and I didn't.

Mike raised an eyebrow at me quizzically.

I nodded slightly in return.

"Whoooaaaaaa!!!" Mike shouted. "Whooooaaaaa baby!!!"

He pulled hard on his rod and whipped the tip frantically. The weight of the dead halibut arched his entire fishing rod nicely.

By reeling hard and then slipping the drag and reeling hard and slipping the drag and shouting and jumping and whipping his fishing rod, Mike managed to make it an exciting fight. He carried on for five minutes.

When Mike finally hauled the fish close to shore, Ralphy—who had lost the coin flip earlier—waded into the pond and thrashed with the halibut, churning water and mud.

"It's a monster, Ricky," he shouted. "Get the bag quick!"

I jumped for the green garbage bag Ralphy had used earlier to carry the halibut.

We fumbled and bobbled the halibut a few times before dropping it into the plastic. Mike grabbed the bag, wrapped it around the fish, then dashed up the bank and quickly slammed the bag into the ground a half dozen times.

"It's a fighter," Mike shouted. "But I think this should quiet him down!"

He sat down and panted. Ralphy climbed onto the bank and shook the water from his clothes. I peeked at Joel.

He was still at the edge of the bank, hunched over his fishing rod. From there, he stared at the bag at Mike's feet in awe. Then Joel jutted his jaw forward, and turned to glare at the pond with new determination.

Hah! I told myself. *We got him! Hook, line, and sinker. He'll never leave this pond until he catches a fish that big. Which will be forever. Hah. Hah—*

That's when fat Mayor Thorpe appeared at the top of the bank, pin-striped suit bulging from his belly. He carried a fishing rod and tackle box.

"Boys," he boomed. "I keep this gear in my office all the time. I hope you don't mind my joining in on the action."

"Let me get this straight," Mike said. "Mayor Thorpe just plopped down and threw his line in the water."

"He could still be there, for all I know," I told him. "If you hadn't run out so quick with the halibut, you wouldn't have to ask."

"Life is cruel, isn't it," was his helpful reply. It was early evening. We had met after supper and were walking to Lisa Higgins' house. Mike nudged Ralphy with his elbow. "I just love that hurt look on his face."

I changed the hurt look to a scowl. "As if I could abandon ship, pal. How was I supposed to know Mayor Thorpe was a fishing nut? He tells me he saw the whole fight—your fight— from his City Hall window. Then his eyes bug out when he sees Joel's fish on that stupid stick and figures two monster fish came from the same pond."

Mike chortled. "I can see it now. What a dilemma. If you tell Mayor Thorpe where Joel really caught that bass, then he'd know about our secret fishing hole. But if you tell Mayor Thorpe that the other fish was only a dead halibut, then Joel would know about our trick." He paused, savoring how I must have squirmed. "How long did you stay?"

"Long enough to whisper and make Joel promise not to say a word to Mayor Thorpe about the bass."

"Um, why not take Joel away with you?" Ralphy asked.

"Are you kidding? It would have taken a tow truck to get him away from the pond. He wanted a fish as big as Mike's. So I left both of them there."

I finally grinned, remembering Joel perched at one end of the pond and Mayor Thorpe hunched over his fishing rod at the other end. Both of them ignored the other as each frantically tried to become the next person to drag a monster fish out of that slimy little pond.

Even without that memory, it was hard to maintain a good scowl for any length of time around my friends. Mike Andrews, in mismatched hightop sneakers and a gaudy Hawaiian shirt that makes your eyes hurt. Red hair. Freckles. The perpetual New York Yankees baseball cap. A grin as wide as a Halloween pumpkin. And born to try anything that looks impossible.

Plus good old Ralphy. Skinny with straight hair that points in all directions. A wrinkled, too-large shirt always hanging out the back of his pants or getting stuck in fences whenever we take shortcuts. In front of a computer, he becomes graceful and confident and serene—a swan on water. Get him away from the computer and sometimes he can be that same swan running on land.

And all three of us terrified of Joel.

As if reading my mind, Ralphy said, "Whatever happens, don't mention any of this to Lisa. She'll never let us forget about Joel's fish or about the mayor."

Mike and I nodded quickly.

Lisa Higgins can be as much trouble as Joel. The only difference being that she's twelve and doesn't have to sneak up on you to drive you nuts. The first problem is that she's pretty. Which catches you off guard once in a while when you're trying to treat her like a pal. She has long dark hair and eyes as blue as the sky. When she smiles, it's warm sunshine breaking through a thunderstorm; when she's mad, it's the thunderstorm itself.

Worse, she's good at sports. What she can't do, she'll practice until she's almost perfect. Like the time Mike teased her about throwing like a girl and she spent two months every day after school pitching a baseball into the playground backstop until she could wing it so hard that the next time Mike caught one from her it sprained two of his fingers.

She was also the reason we were going to San Diego.

Her uncle, Carl Lovelee, had just moved there from Hollywood into a big old house. Lisa was his favorite niece—we told her it was because she was his only niece—and he had asked her to find some friends to help him paint it. So she elected us. Not that we fought hard to get out of that.

The trip, of course, had been all we could think of for the last while. As we rounded the corner that led to the Higgins' house, Mike spoke quietly.

"Remember, guys, not much talk about Lisa's uncle in front of her dad. We've heard his lecture enough times."

Carl Lovelee was Lisa's mother's brother. And, especially with what he did for a living, he wasn't popular with Mr. Higgins.

We began to pass under the huge elm tree in the Higgins' front yard, and as he closed the gate, Ralphy shook his head. "How could anyone who is nice enough to send all of us plane tickets"—Oh no! I began to elbow Ralphy in warning as a movement caught the corner of my eye, but it was too late—"be half as bad as Lisa's dad says he—Ow, Ricky! What'd you do that for!"

"Hi, Mr. Higgins," Mike said without hope in his voice as he too noticed the movement. "Um, trimming branches tonight?"

Ralphy gulped with awareness.

Mr. Higgins pursed his lips. "Logically, one would assume so, as one sees me with these clippers and as one also sees me standing on this ladder with said clippers in hand and freshly snipped branches on the grass beneath said ladder. Although, I might add, one did not see me soon enough to prevent me from hearing Ralphy's verbal assertation."

Mr. Higgins was a lawyer. And deputy mayor, a part-time job in a small town like Jamesville.

"Yes, sir," Mike said. "When you put it that way . . ."

Suddenly, Mr. Higgins laughed. "Come up to the house, guys. I'll see if I can round us up some lemonade."

The three of us exchanged startled glances as Mr. Higgins climbed down the ladder. He was a wiry man, with thinning gray hair and stern features. That was the first time we had heard him laugh. And also the first time he had called us "guys" instead of "young men."

"Maybe he won a lottery," Ralphy whispered.

"No," Mike whispered back, "maybe it's a twin brother. One with a sense of humor."

As he marched, and without turning his head, Mr. Higgins calmly said, "A little more respect, young men. Although I'm losing my hair, I'm not deaf. Your curiosity will be satisfied soon enough."

All three of us turned red.

Once in the kitchen, he whistled as he poured us lemonade, and then motioned us into chairs. "Lisa," he called, "your friends are here. And I have news for all of you."

He's canceled the trip, I thought with despair. *He dislikes Carl Lovelee so much that he finally decided to cancel the trip and it's put him into a good mood.*

Lisa entered the kitchen with a puzzled look on her face—which only got more puzzled when she saw the beaming joy on her father's face—and took a chair beside the three of us.

"First of all," Mr. Higgins began, "I don't have to tell you what I think of Lisa's uncle, Carl Lovelee."

He was absolutely right. He didn't have to tell us. That didn't stop him. We heard—again—how Carl Lovelee had deliberately turned his back on work for years and years. How he deliberately mocked everything that proper society stood for. How, at age fifty, he still refused to grow up. And worst of all, how, by selling to Hollywood his first rotten, incomprehensible screenplay, he had made more money than Mr. Higgins could make with fifteen years of respectable lawyering.

Mr. Higgins paused for breath. Then smiled triumphantly. "But we'll see who has the last laugh."

I finally dared to ask, "You're not changing your mind about letting Lisa and the rest of us go to California, are you sir?"

Mr. Higgins snorted. "No. Much as I dislike her brother, I do love Mrs. Higgins. And if she insists it will be good for Lisa to visit, then . . ."

I breathed a sigh of relief and took my first sip of lemonade.

Mr. Higgins smiled to himself. "Yes sir, we'll see who has the last laugh when all of you show up in San Diego. I almost wish I could be there to see it."

"Dad," Lisa protested, "what is going on?"

His smile widened. "Let me have a little fun. Just for a while, Lisa. I saw something today that made me laugh so hard, I feel ten years younger."

We waited.

"Don't you want to ask?" he demanded.

When his features threatened to become stern, we nodded.

The smile returned. Mr. Higgins slapped his thigh and nearly giggled. "I saw that plump mayor of ours fishing in the mud hole beside City Hall! He's now the laughing stock of the town!"

I wanted to faint.

Mr. Higgins slapped his thigh again. "Better yet, he did it because of a six-year-old kid."

I really wanted to faint.

Mr. Higgins thought the pain on my face was disbelief. "That's right," he insisted. "In fact, it was your brother, Ricky. Oh, it's too rich. Too rich indeed. A six-year-old kid making a fool out of our mayor. And I don't have to tell you what I think of him, do I."

Mr. Higgins then explained how many times he and Mayor Thorpe had disagreed when it was quite obvious Mayor Thorpe was totally wrong.

My stomach hurt with worry. Mayor Thorpe was probably on

the telephone right now, calling our parents because of the trick we had played. *Hold it*, I told myself. Maybe we weren't in total trouble. Mr. Higgins hadn't mentioned us. Yet.

Ralphy must have been just as worried. "Um, how do you know it was only—" he blurted, then caught himself. "I mean, how do you know it was Joel who fooled him?"

"Any lawyer can put facts together," came the assured reply. "From my law-office window around mid-morning, I happened to see your brother carrying a big fish on a stick. He was obviously headed in the direction of the park, although why he was sneaking behind cars and bushes is beyond me. Second of all, at lunch time, I saw that same fish on the same stick beside him as he fished in the little mud hole. Ergo, that fish wasn't caught in that pond. But Mayor Thorpe fell for it hook, line, and sinker. I hear he stayed there all day and sunburned himself as red as an apple! Imagine that, letting a little kid sucker you so badly in front of all Jamesville."

"Imagine that, sir," I said.

"But Dad," Lisa said. "What could this possibly have to do with Uncle Carl?"

"Oh, nothing," Mr. Higgins said. "Nothing at all."

He permitted himself a satisfied smile. "Except, of course, I know Ricky's parents and I've heard more than one story about that Joel character and his teddy bear. So, with the permission of Ricky's mother, I took the liberty of making certain arrangements. I don't even mind paying the extra plane fare myself."

"I beg your pardon, sir," I said.

"Yes, Ricky. Lisa's Uncle Carl is going to have the pleasure of meeting your wonderful little brother. Anybody who can fool Mayor Thorpe is welcome to do the same to that scoundrel Carl Lovelee."

A wave of doom roared in my ears.

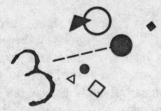

We had only one hope of containing Joel in San Diego. His teddy bear.

I held it firmly in my lap as our plane began to descend. The teddy bear was battered brown with gray-white paws and a white button for the left eye and a black button for the right eye. Not the type of thing you'd expect a kid as terrifying as Joel to need as a security blanket. But it was his only weak point.

When Joel sleeps, you can steamroll a marching band through his room at top volume and he won't stir. Yet wriggle one paw of his teddy bear, and he wakes instantly to stare at you with accusing eyes. He becomes a nervous wreck if he loses sight of it.

Joel patted my knee with brotherly love and looked at his bear. I stared over Joel's head to soak in the view.

Maybe I should have been too scared to enjoy looking out. After all, the plane was—as Mike had said again and again—nearly a hundred tons of steel and explosive fuel rushing through the air at more than five hundred miles an hour. From our cruising altitude some six miles above the ground, if the engines had quit—as Mike had delighted in pointing out a dozen times during our flight—we would have glided downward with as much grace as a dropped piano. It's not the kind of conversation that makes flying with a guy like Mike very easy.

But I wasn't nervous. Not that my prayer at the beginning of the flight was something for good luck. It was much more. Some-

times, as Dad often told me, you forget God during ordinary days.
So there was nothing like fear to remind you to remember whose
hands you were in, and how much that meant. Which always
made for a good time to pray—and I had—earlier, when we'd
been sitting on the runway waiting for the jet engines to warm
before takeoff.

So now, instead of cringing nervously as we circled to land, I
was hungry to see as much as possible. The land, looming fast
as we dropped, unfolded to become dusty brown canyons dotted
with hillside houses. We circled west into the afternoon sun and
the brown-green horizon became a dazzling blue of sky meeting
ocean. Then the glass and concrete of downtown San Diego.

"Pretty bridge," Joel said.

It was pretty. A thin highway cut across a large bay and rose
steeply in the middle where ships could pass beneath.

Ralphy leaned between the seats and said, "It's the Coronado
Bridge."

"Like, you've been here before?" Mike asked with disbelief in
his voice.

"No," Ralphy said, "But those of us who can read also know
maps are handy to look at before traveling."

"Hmmph."

As we swooped down, it seemed that the highest pillars of the
bridge would knock a wing off. Of course they didn't, and we
rushed past the huge gray Navy ships in the harbor, and then
with scarcely a bump, we were safely on the runway.

"Guys," Lisa said, "welcome to Southern California."

I grinned with relief. With Joel, there was potential for trouble
anywhere. Even on a four-hour flight. So far he hadn't done
anything.

* * * * * * * *

"I don't see Uncle Carl," Lisa said. "And it's been at least five
minutes." She anxiously shifted her weight from foot to foot.

Mike spoke in a dry voice. "Your dad predicted he would be late. What were the words he used? *Unreliable, forgetful, shifty —* "

"Don't worry, Lisa," I said before Mike got into full gear. "I'm sure he'll be here. You can stop hopping like a frog in a frying pan."

She turned red. "Actually, it's something else. We had a lot of pop and juice on the plane and something about those tiny washrooms at the back was so scary that . . ."

"Oh."

Mike, who hates waiting in any situation, said, "Why don't you go to where you need to go. We'll get the luggage and meet you back here. With any bit of luck, your uncle will show up by then."

Since it had been thirty seconds since I had last scanned the reception area of the airport gate, I spoke loudly without turning my head. "Joel, get back here. Or your teddy gets strangled."

Joel glided back into sight.

"Stay close," I told him. "This is a big airport, and you're a small kid."

"I'll be right back," Lisa promised as she left.

Mike and Ralphy and I followed signs to the baggage claim area. Joel trailed behind us. I dangled his teddy bear in plain sight from my right hand. It was embarrassing but worth it. Joel didn't dare stray.

Our luggage was there already, even all of our skateboards, and we soon were headed back to the gate to meet Lisa. Joel insisted on carrying his suitcase, and that slowed us a little.

Halfway to the gate area, we turned a corner and almost stumbled into the back of a woman squatting down to tie her shoelaces. Strangely, she wore a cap which covered all of her hair except for the long and narrow ponytail which hung straight down and almost touched the floor as she squatted.

"Sorry, ma'am," Mike said.

The woman stood and turned. It was a New York Yankees baseball cap that she wore. Just like Mike's.

"No problem, kid," came the reply with a grin. "And let me commend you on a great choice of head gear."

We were too stunned to say a word.

He was no woman.

He had an almost triangular face that made him look fox-like, especially with his pointed goatee. He was tall and wore a baggy sweatshirt, sleeves cut off ragged at the shoulders. His pants were white cotton, and when I looked down, I saw that instead of tying shoelaces, he must have been adjusting straps, because he wore sandals. He looked nearly as old as my grandfather.

We stepped back. We were definitely not in the presence of a normal grown-up. The surprise must have shown on our faces.

"You kids got some money for a starving ex-hippie?" he asked. "Spare change or anything?"

I quickly dug into my pockets and gave him what I could. I wanted out of there.

Mike and Ralphy hurried behind me, and we didn't dare look back.

"They told me California was crazy," Mike said in a whisper. "But did we have to find out so soon?"

I nodded. "As long as he doesn't follow us. He sure looked creepy in a ponytail."

We were almost to the gate area, and I was just beginning to scan for Lisa and, hopefully, her uncle, when my own words clicked. *Follow us.* As in *Joel had better be following us.*

I turned. Naturally, he was nowhere in sight.

"Nuts," I said. "We shouldn't have gone so fast. Joel couldn't keep up."

I set my luggage down and trudged to the last corner we had rounded.

I couldn't believe my eyes! The middle-aged hippie was wrestling Joel for his suitcase!

"Mike! Ralphy!" That was all I said before sprinting to rescue Joel.

I didn't give myself time to think. Middle-aged or not, he was a big man, and desperate enough to try robbing a small kid. I dodged an old lady and her leashed poodle, and as I dove at the hippie, I grabbed for the first thing that flashed into sight. His ponytail.

It brought him crashing down beside me as we tumbled into a pile beside Joel. I tried a punch, but it didn't work. He caught my fist and held it. It seemed to freeze us. The strange part was his face. Calm and strong.

I said nothing, but tried to swing with my other hand. He caught that too, and I was helpless.

Then Mike and Ralphy arrived, bowling both of us over in their mad rush to rescue me. Mike managed to pin down the hippy's shoulders and Ralphy sat on his legs.

Weirdly, the hippie stopped struggling and only smiled.

"I'll get Security," I panted. "He was trying to take Joel's suitcase and—"

Lisa interrupted from behind us. "I got here as quick as I could! I saw you guys walk around the corner, drop your luggage and run back here, and—"

I interrupted her. "Quick. Get Security. Or even your uncle. We've got this guy trapped and—"

Lisa moaned. "Let him go."

"What? He tried robbing Joel."

Her eyes became steel. "Let him go."

Mike rolled off his shoulders. Ralphy moved off his legs.

The hippie stood and dusted himself. "Not bad work, guys. Somewhat misguided, but not bad work at all. And by the way, let me introduce myself."

He stuck out a hand. "The name's Lovelee. Carl Lovelee."

From the passenger side of Carl's Jeep, I had much more time to study him. We were driving along Interstate 5, a freeway that followed the base of canyon hills. The top of the Jeep was off, and warm air blew over the windshield and rushed across our faces.

Carl smiled peacefully at the traffic around us.

"About fifteen minutes till we get there," he said, raising his voice above the buffeting wind to call out to Lisa, Ralphy, Mike, and Joel who sat on the back bench of the Jeep. Carl's long ponytail was tucked behind his back and pressed against the seat as he drove. The rest of his face around the goatee was clean shaven. The skin around the eyes and the corners of his mouth was lined deeply to match the features of his smile. Cobalt blue eyes and strong white teeth. Watching him, I wondered how I could have mistaken him for a creep.

"Did I pass inspection?" he asked casually.

"What's that?" Mike leaned forward between the seats.

"I was speaking to your friend," Carl said. "I think he understands."

I did. My face was burning red. Mike sat back.

Carl said nothing until he began to slow for an exit. GRAND AVENUE, 1/2 MILE, the sign read, LA JOLLA AND MISSION BEACH WEST.

"What color is that Camaro in front of us?" The question was directed to me.

I looked back at Mike and Ralphy and Lisa. They shrugged. "Yellow," I said.

Carl merely nodded and hummed until we reached Grand Avenue. We had to wait at a red light.

"What color is that house?" He again directed his question to me as he pointed to a large bungalow on the side of the hill in front of us.

What did he think I was? Stupid?

"White," I said. I was getting ready to again think he was a weird creep.

"I think I'll take a short detour," he announced as the light turned green.

Carl turned onto a small side street that wound its way up the hill and brought us to the white bungalow.

He stopped in front of it and calmly gazed at the white exterior until all of us, restless, shifted in our seats.

"White," he stated.

Then he put the Jeep into gear and turned into a small alley. He drove slowly until we reached the back of the house, painted a brilliant pink.

"Would you say the house is white?" he asked me.

I shook my head.

"Just curious, of course," he said and accelerated.

We drove in silence for another five minutes, reaching Grand Avenue and turning west to head to the ocean. It gave me time to think.

So when Carl asked, "What color is that Corvette?" I had an answer ready for him.

"The side that I can see is red."

He laughed suddenly. "Exactly! That, almost, is my entire lesson on appearances."

"First," Carl pointed to our right, "my house is up the hill from here in an area called La Jolla —" he pronounced it "La Hoya" — "but I'd like to stop at the beach first. I need to meet someone."

"La Hoya?" Mike repeated. "I thought it was La Jolla." Mike pronounced it with a *J* and a double *L*.

Once again, Carl said nothing. He waited until we had found a parking spot a few minutes later.

He pulled a brown paper lunch bag from under his seat, before holding the steering wheel in his left hand for support and shifting around to face Mike in the back. With his right hand, the one nearest me, Carl kept a casual grip on the paper bag which he balanced on his knee.

Then he said, "Mike, in Spanish the *J* is pronounced as our *H*. And a double *L* is pronounced a *Y*. It fits in with what I was trying to prove about the house you all thought was white." He paused. "Things are rarely as they appear to be. Assumptions without logic can be dangerous."

I tried not to stare at the small rip in the bottom corner of the lunch bag.

Carl remained in his half turned position, unaware of what I could see sticking out the rip.

"The obvious example," Carl continued, "is the reason the three of you jumped me in the airport. Joel dropped his suitcase and it fell apart. Yet when you saw me snapping it shut while Joel held it together, you assumed something much different. And the reason you made that assumption was based on another false assumption about my appearance."

"Well, sir," Mike said, "you did ask us for money."

My mind raced through possibilities for what I saw as they spoke, but I found nothing I liked.

"My sense of humor," Carl explained. "It's an immediate reaction when people stare at me like I'm a refugee from the hippie days of the '60s."

Ralphy spoke shyly. "But you do look like that with your sandals and ponytail and little beard."

Despite the people ahead of us on the beach, I was still staring at the bag, barely aware of the conversation around me.

At Ralphy's question, Carl suddenly tightened his grip on the bag. His knuckles whitened almost instantly. His other hand clenched hard around the steering wheel. "You're right, of course." Then he smiled sadly as his fingers relaxed. "Believe me, there are days I wish I could wear a brushcut."

Later, I realized I should have listened more closely. But my attention, like my eyes, was riveted on the lunch bag.

Carl spoke, his voice empty. "Someday, I might tell all of you how not to make a terrible mistake. But until then—"

Sudden silence. It made me feel like a daydreamer caught in class by the teacher. Carl's eyes shifted from my face to what I had been staring at. He said nothing more, only tucked the bag under his shirt and let himself out of the Jeep.

"Surf's up," he called to us and began to walk toward the beach without waiting.

"What was all that about?" Mike whispered when we were stepping out of the Jeep.

I kept my voice low. "Let me tell you later. But do me a favor. Keep a close eye on who Carl meets or what he does with the bag. I'm going to take Joel down the water and pretend nothing is wrong. Whatever you do, don't say anything to Lisa."

Mike noticed the seriousness on my face and nodded.

Salt was in the air, thick enough to taste, just as I had imagined it would be. The waves crashed in low booms the way I had dreamed they would in Southern California. Sand, screaming gulls, and the bright colors of crowds of people. But I felt lousy.

The rip in Carl's lunch bag had been wide enough to show layers of paper bills. Tens and twenties. And I couldn't convince myself that Lisa's crazy uncle had come to the beach to make a bank deposit.

"By the way," Carl said as he set a casserole down in front of us for supper that night, "you might find it a note of historical interest that the unofficial name of the area around this house is 'Pirate's Haven.' "

"Pirate's Haven!" Ralphy squeaked.

I said nothing. The paper bag with money was bothering me too much. Mike and I had not had a chance to speak alone, so I had no idea what Carl had done with the cash. What made me more uncomfortable was Carl's wise, humorous eyes and his gentle way of speaking. It was too easy to like him, and I didn't want to. Not with the mystery of the paper bag unsolved. Not with Carl's own advice about appearances.

Carl grinned at Ralphy. "Thought that might get your attention." He spooned out heaps of steaming noodles onto our plates.

"Pray, Joel," I whispered before he could dig in.

Carl opened his mouth to say something, then thought better of it as Joel's eyes sparkled at the importance of his job.

When Joel finished asking the blessing on the food for all of us, Carl started eating.

"Come on," Lisa begged. "You can't stop your story now."

"Oh, yes," Carl teased. "The Pirate's Haven story. I thought you'd never ask."

The noodles were covered with a white cream sauce that buried chunks and chunks of large shrimp. With fresh, hot bread, the meal was delicious.

"In the mid 1800s, the story is told, Manuel Allegro Torres and his band of thieves began raiding the small settlements up and down the coast. They were common horseback bandits, quite good at what they did, with one small difference. Manuel Allegro Torres became known as the Gentleman Pirate because he insisted that no one be killed during his raids. Other bandits were not as considerate back then."

"Horses? I thought you said he was a pirate," Lisa said.

Carl nodded as he worked on a mouthful of noodles. "It was much more practical back then to rob settlements on horseback. What made Manuel the Gentleman Pirate so successful was that he moved his entire gang and all their horses up and down the coast by ship. They would dock somewhere, make a lightning raid on an unsuspecting settlement, blaze back to the ship, raise anchor, and disappear on the ocean. They always returned to their safe spot, here. Tomorrow, when you visit the cliffs, you'll see how he managed to hide his ship for so many years."

"Is this true?" Ralphy asked. "I mean, you do write screenplays and ... "

Carl laughed. "Good point. I'm supposed to make up stories. Let me assure you, what I relate about the Pirate's Haven is what is actually in the legend. As to the truth of the legend, I cannot make any judgments. I can only tell you that this house was Manuel's original house. That fact, plus the difficulty of finding his anchored ship, led to people naming it the Pirate's Haven."

"How about buried treasure?" Ralphy blurted. "Don't most pirate legends have buried treasure?"

Carl doffed an imaginary hat in grave respect to Ralphy. "Thank you for a shining example of a logical assumption. Yes, like most pirate legends, the one of Manuel the Gentleman Pirate involves buried treasure. And I expect to make a lot of money as a result of it."

Mike's eyes grew wide. "You flew us here to help you search for buried treasure!"

Once again Carl laughed. "That, Mike, is a shining example of a wrong assumption. You're here simply because this old house needs a lot of painting and it was a good excuse to bring Lisa and a few of her friends here. On the other hand, looking for buried treasure that may or may not exist is highly speculative and rarely fruitful. But writing a screenplay about it is a different story altogether."

"Since we're speaking of puns," Lisa interrupted with a cute smile on her face, "could you call our work here 'manual' labor?"

I barely heard them. My mind was busy on trying to see the real Carl. Was he trying to convince us he could afford to fly us here by being a respectable screenwriter? What story would he use to explain dealings on the beach with bags of money?

"But there is buried treasure," Mike insisted.

"As legend has it, gold coins and jewels that represent most of all he robbed," Carl replied. "Legend also has it that Manuel drew a map and put it—" he scratched his goatee "—what is that phrase? Oh yes. 'In the sight of all who care to open their eyes at the break of summer dawn.' "

"Too cool!" Mike said. "Someone wake me up early tomorrow."

"Don't worry," Carl said. "I certainly will. You guys have a lot of sanding ahead of you. I think a fair way is this. Mornings you're on my time. Afternoons are all yours." He looked at Joel. "Even you, my unexpected guest. I suspect I shall have to keep a close eye on you."

He doesn't know how true that is, I said to myself. Joel is at his innocent and ghostly worst when a person is doing something he'd rather not get caught at.

But I said out loud, "How come you know so much about the legend?"

Carl smiled. "Research for the screenplay. In fact, the historian who so kindly supplied me with much of what I know is arriving tomorrow. This house is certainly big enough."

A sudden thought hit me, one that had been nagging during

the talk about renovations. Maybe Carl wanted kids to help him renovate because he was afraid that adults might spot the buried treasure. Or—if he was up to anything criminal—his real activities.

I vowed to be on guard for anything.

* * * * * * *

Carl was right about one thing. The house was definitely big enough.

Three stories high, it seemed to have hundreds of rooms. The outside walls, I had noticed as we drove up late in the afternoon, were made of large square bricks handcrafted—as Carl had explained—by Mexicans and shipped up the coast.

The inside hallways were wide enough to be runways. Cool tile floors. High arched ceilings with slow-moving fans. Large windows. Stately furniture. The stairs leading to the second floor bedrooms were curved, with wood banisters.

Carl had a master bedroom with a large study attached to it. Lisa's room was at that end of the house.

Between those rooms and ours were a library, another study, two empty rooms, and another stairway leading to the third floor. At our end of the house, Mike and Ralphy had a room opposite the one Joel and I shared.

As soon as the house was quiet, and Joel's breathing had become long and deep from sleep, I moved across the hallway, grateful for a floor that did not creak.

Mike's bedroom door opened soundlessly.

Faint moonlight shone through their window. I tiptoed to one bed and shook Mike's shoulder. I thought.

"Eeep!"

"Sorry, Ralphy."

By the time I got to Mike's bed, he was sitting upright. "I was wondering when you'd get here," he said.

"Well, you could have told me he was coming," Ralphy mumbled to Mike as he struggled to breathe normally. "I was nearly asleep and dreaming about pirate ghosts when he grabbed my shoulder."

"Forget pirate's ghosts," I whispered as I quietly pulled a chair to sit between both beds. "Lisa's uncle may be much more trouble."

"What!" Ralphy hiccupped once, something he tends to do when he gets flustered.

"Shhh. Mike, what did you see when you followed Carl?"

"Uh-uh," he said. "First you tell me what was in that bag."

"No way. First you tell me what you saw."

The silence that followed lengthened into minutes.

More silence. Then a light clunk on the floor at my feet.

"What was that?" Mike asked.

"A coin," Ralphy replied. "The suspense was killing me. Heads, Ricky goes first. Tails, Mike reports. And . . ." Ralphy scrambled from the covers to squint in the light of the moon. . . "it's heads."

"OK," I said. "When Carl was explaining Spanish spelling to you guys in the jeep, I noticed a rip in the paper bag he carried. It was full of money."

"Get out of town!" Mike said. "No way."

"Sure, Mike. I'm making this up."

He whistled a low whistle. "That would explain a lot. You see, following Carl wasn't easy. As soon as he met someone, they both went into a beach restaurant. I couldn't go inside to watch."

"Who was it?" I demanded.

"I forgot to ask him for his driver's license," Mike said.

I sighed. "What did he look like?"

"Tall. Way taller than Carl. Brushcut. And one other thing that will make it easy to remember. He had an eyepatch."

"You waited, of course, until they came out of the restaurant."

"Of course. Except Carl came out first and alone, so I followed him back to where you guys were on the beach. If I would have known that the two of you would be sitting beside three gorgeous lifeguards while I was slaving away at detective work—"

"We had our spot first," Ralphy insisted. "They showed up after. Really. Lisa moved between them and us anyway and—"

"Mike," I interrupted. "Was Carl carrying anything when he left the restaurant?"

"Nothing I could see." Obviously, Mike was remembering Carl's lessons on observation.

"That's not good," I said. "In everything you read or everything you see on television, big cash deals mean something crooked. And if Carl was carrying a package too small to see . . ."

"I was afraid you would say that," Ralphy said. "And here I was looking forward to a peaceful sleep."

"What could it be?" Mike leaned forward as he spoke. Even as he leaned forward, I knew he was afraid to say it first.

So I did. "Drugs. The one thing a person hates to think about is . . ."

"Drugs," Ralphy whispered. "It's a terrible thought. But most of the time on television those deals are drugs."

"It would explain why he has enough money to buy a house like this," I pointed out. "But for Lisa's sake, let's pray not."

When I returned to my room, I was relieved to see Joel still there, sleeping soundly. The last thing I needed was for him to disappear. It looked like I had enough to worry about already.

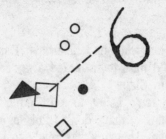

"You're an atheist, aren't you?" I said.

Carl look startled. We were alone, sitting on the back veranda and cleaning some paint brushes just before lunch. My second day in California and I was speckled white from Mike's habit of putting too much paint on his brush and then wielding it like a madman.

"An atheist," Carl repeated. "Someone who doesn't believe in God. Why would you ask that?"

"It's a hunch," I said levelly, surprised at my calm boldness. "The way you looked at Joel when he prayed at supper last night. The way you insist on logic. And sometimes you seem so . . ." I searched for a word to describe Carl's detachment from things.

"So resigned to life? So uninvolved with emotions?"

I nodded. I couldn't say how or why I got that impression. It wasn't just the possibility that he dealt drugs. It was just the way he seemed to stand back from us with a tiny amused quirk on his face that sometimes looked wise and gentle and sometimes looked sad despite his efforts to hide it.

"I'll have to watch my step around you," Carl said slowly. He then added, "Yes, I am an atheist. If you are a believer, though, I hope that doesn't discourage you from your beliefs."

The way he looked at me steadily, I knew it wasn't time for a kid-and-grown-up talk, the ones where you have to watch what you say so the grown-up doesn't get mad.

So I said, "If you really don't think God is there, why should you be worried about whether I believe in Him or not?"

He shrugged. "I'd hate to take God away from you, the way they did with Santa Claus."

Obviously, he wasn't going to pull punches either. Some grown-ups figure kids our age don't think or have questions or opinions of our own. This one was ready to talk.

I replied, "God's too big to take away or return." I paused as a thought hit me. "And Santa Claus doesn't have a book like the Bible to describe himself."

"Aren't you a little young to be so sure of these things?"

"Aren't you a little old to not know these things?" It came out quickly, and I expected him to get mad.

Instead, he smiled sadly. "Maybe. But remember the house you thought was white yesterday? In other words, don't make assumptions on what you see. Or in this case, what you don't see."

He gave me some silence. I looked across the back of his yard to the wire fence that ran across the top of the cliffs. Beyond it, the ocean. I struggled for the right words to say, the ones that I knew were there.

This is what came out. "My dad told me if once you accepted God and—pardon me for saying the next part—because he also said it took a strong fool not to accept God—then the rest made sense. I only wish I knew enough more to say it the way my dad does."

Silence from Carl, and the same sad smile.

I had a sudden thought. "Carl, how far to the moon?"

He stared at me. "Two-hundred-and-fifty-thousand miles."

I took a breath before plunging in. "Did you measure that yourself?"

"No. But—"

I then knew what I was getting at. "You haven't seen it for yourself. In other words, despite your best logic, you've taken that knowledge on faith."

"That's different," he protested. "Other people have measured it. Scientists. They've written it down, passed it on."

"Other people have known God's presence. They've written it down, passed it on."

Carl burst out laughing. "I can't believe this. You hung me on my own rope. A twelve-year-old!"

I couldn't believe it myself. For a few minutes, I had felt strong and mature. If only it could have lasted during the week, we might not have gotten into trouble.

Then Carl sobered his laugh and stood abruptly, still holding the paint brushes in one hand. "I believed in God once. A long time ago." He tugged on his ponytail with his other hand. "Then came the reason for this."

I waited for him to continue.

He didn't. He set the brushes down on the old newspaper beside our chairs. Then walked back into the house.

* * * * * * * *

Carl did not mention our conversation during lunch. And I didn't ask him about the ponytail.

As we finished eating, he told us we were on our own for the afternoon and asked one simple question. It was the one simple question I didn't like. "Where's Joel?"

I groaned. *Gone. His teddy bear gone too.* Which meant he could be lurking anywhere, and us without any way of controlling him.

Mike said, "The best way to look for Joel is to try to find some privacy. Presto, he'll be there."

Too true. With that, Mike, Ralphy, Lisa, and I trooped out of the kitchen to look around the neighborhood. Our first stop was the back gate of Carl's wire fence, the back gate that opened to the top of the cliffs.

We stopped beyond it and admired the view. Far below us — probably a hundred feet beneath our feet — the ocean waves rose and fell.

In both directions away from us, the fenced properties of other houses followed the line of the cliffs. From each yard, crooked footpaths angled down the face of the cliffs. We could see that the climbs were not impossible. Only difficult.

Each footpath ended below at the narrow strip of sand that ran in a long ribbon along the base of the cliffs. We stood in the breeze that came in from the ocean and stared down for a long time.

Finally, Lisa softly broke the silence. "So that's why they call it Pirate's Haven."

The rest of us only nodded. A couple hundred yards offshore, a huge rock broke from the surface of the water. Its height reached three quarters the height of the cliffs. Its length looked longer than a football field. And almost in its center on the side facing us was the Pirate's Haven. A small natural harbor cut sharply into the rock.

"No wonder they couldn't find the ship of the Gentleman Pirate," Ralphy said. "Searchers passing by on the other side would assume the rock is solid all the way through."

"Exactly," Mike said. "The perfect parking stall."

That it was. The entire rock must have been far enough offshore to ensure the water was deep enough for a ship to enter the tiny harbor.

Mike continued. "Let's go down."

"Slowly," Ralphy added.

"Hah!" I said. "Joel's afraid of heights. He'll never follow us down. And you know what this means . . ." I waggled my eyebrows significantly at Lisa until she giggled. ". . . For the rest of our vacation, we can lose him anytime we want by heading down the cliffs."

Mike and Ralphy grinned. For good reasons over the years, they've learned to be as terrified of Joel as I am.

Right then, I tried not to worry about Joel. Sure, he had disappeared right as lunch ended. But he was, after all, Joel, and disappearing was his usual method of locomotion. I didn't have to worry about his safety either. To him, this was new territory, so he wouldn't stray far from Carl's house. It was a nice neighborhood anyway, filled with houses as big as Carl's.

In fact, I forgot about Joel until we discovered Carl's next-door neighbor.

Our first warning was a scuffle slightly below us and around a bend. Then a sharp *clink clink*. A quick thud. Slight grunting. A louder scuffle. A *whoosh*. A spraying thump. Then silence for five seconds before the next light scuffle.

Mike, in front, looked back and frowned. We all stopped in midstep.

We listened through several more cycles. The only thing that changed was the clinking. Twice it was there, and twice it wasn't.

"Horseshoes?" Mike whispered.

"Sure, Mike. Played by pink elephants in ballerina outfits."

He scowled at me. "OK, Sherlock," he whispered again, "you tell us."

Lisa tapped my shoulder. "It's someone digging," she said in a low voice.

I listened again. Her theory made sense. I whispered ahead to Mike. "Sounds like someone digging." Mike just shook his head in disgust at me and mouthed a "thank you" to Lisa.

We crept ahead. Ralphy moved from ahead of me and Lisa to behind me and Lisa. We rounded the bend almost on our hands and knees.

Mike, still in front, saw her first. When he stood, it caught the rest of us off guard. But when we, too, reached him, we understood why there was no need to hide. It was a tiny lady in a baggy dark dress. Beside her was a full potato sack.

"Hello, ma'am," Mike said. I could hear the grin in his voice as he spoke. It's a grin that's earned him chocolate chip cookies from aunts and grandmas all across Jamesville.

She stopped shovelling halfway through a toss, looked up, and squinted through wire-frame glasses perched on a tiny nose. She looked to be about Carl's age. Her hair was streaked with gray and pulled tight in a prim bun. She seemed so frail that her shovel dwarfed her.

"Nice afternoon, isn't it ma'am," Mike continued, his charm in top form.

"It was until you little idiots showed up," she said with a glare. "And wipe that stupid grin off your face. You're fooling nobody."

With that, she gave a healthy spit into the hole she had been digging.

Mike staggered a half step back.

"No reason for the pack of you to stand there staring. Scram. Vamoose. Find a video game or whatever it is hooligans do these days."

"Hooligans?" Mike began. I could hear the grin going back into his voice again. "Ma'am—"

"Didn't I tell you that face of yours looked stupid with a grin plastered all over it? Now move along."

Her glare worsened.

I looked for a way to ease the tension. "Aren't you worried about the cliff breaking away on you?" I asked politely.

"I've been digging holes for my kitty litter for nearly thirty years now, sonny. Don't give me any bunk about unstable cliffs."

"Kitty litter?" Lisa echoed.

"It's good for the ecology. I really care about Mother Earth. Unlike—" The lady's face softened. She pushed her glasses up her nose and squinted again. "Why, you're a girl. Sometimes I can't tell with the way kids do their hair these days. You should see the old geezer who moved in next door to me. He's got a ponytail to make a woman cry with jealousy."

Lisa giggled. "That's my Uncle Carl. He's a screenwriter. He used to live in Hollywood."

"Hmmph," the lady snorted. "Don't think I don't see him

coming and going at all hours of the night. It makes my cats jumpy. Tell him Doreen said to knock it off."

All hours of the night!

Lisa missed my sideways glance at Ralphy. She said, "I love cats."

"Well, so do I, missy. So you can tell your gang of friends to stay away from the house."

I looked closer at the potato bag near the hole. There actually was kitty litter spilling slightly from the top. "Exactly how many cats do you have?" I asked.

She focused her glare on me, then straightened proudly. "Fifty-two."

"That's nice," I said. *Was she a lunatic?*

"Don't you get any strange ideas about tormenting my babies," she said as her glare returned.

"You have babies too?" Ralphy asked. I elbowed him. Sometimes I don't know if he's joking or just temporarily vacant.

"Don't get smart with me, young man. Or I'll sic Hezekiah on you."

I was ready to be vacant myself. We run into a grouchy cat lady on the side of a cliff burying twenty pounds of used cat litter and she threatens to sic a dog named Hezekiah on us. This, of course, is after a theological debate with a man old enough to be my grandfather who may be a drug dealer and who also has a ponytail to his waist. So much for my daydreams about Southern California.

Then, despite the heat of the sun, I broke into a cold sweat.

"Fifty-two cats, ma'am? Right next door to Carl?"

"You deaf? Or just slow?"

I ignored the insult. Fifty-two cats next door and Joel on the loose. That was like aiming a hot blow torch at gunpowder.

"Just how big is Hezekiah?" I asked, my throat tightening in dismay at a picture of a huge dog guarding all those cats.

"Twenty-three pounds of claws and teeth. The meanest tomcat

alive. And don't you forget it."

"We won't, ma'am," I said quickly. Just a dumb cat. Nothing to worry about. Still, I gritted my teeth at nightmare thoughts of Joel's exact activities at the moment. Us safe for the rest of our vacation? Hah! I should have known better. If only Mr. Higgins knew who he had really punished by sending Joel along.

Under my breath, I said to Lisa, "She likes you. Please, please hang around and talk. I need time to find Joel."

Lisa nodded slightly. Mike and I left her and Ralphy to argue with Doreen the cat lady.

Once out of sight, I began scrambling up the path as fast as I could. The coughs behind me meant Mike was staying close, in my dust. We reached the summit and I stopped to pant for breath.

"He could be anywhere, Mike," I said with urgency. I had visions of dozens of police cars pulling up to investigate the ruckus Joel could have caused by now. "And we probably don't have long until Doreen gets back to her house. Let's split up."

Mike grinned. "Don't worry any more, pal. You got your buddy to help you out. I'll whistle if I find Joel before you do." As Mike walked away, I heard him laughing to himself. "Hezekiah the guard cat," he chortled. "Scary stuff."

Five minutes later Mike's sharp whistle pierced my panic. I wanted to faint with relief. Instead, I sprinted back to Carl's yard. Mike arrived shortly after, slowly walking with Joel beside him.

In one hand, he held Joel's hand. In the other, he held Joel's teddy bear.

As Mike came closer, I saw the reason for his slowness. Four long deep gashes ran parallel in perfectly straight lines down his left cheek.

"I don't want to talk about it," he said flatly. "Ever."

It was making me sick to watch Mike wince bravely every time Lisa dabbed the moist facecloth against the scratches on his cheek.

"Mike, your face hasn't been this clean in years. Don't you think enough is enough?"

Instead of a reply, he yelped convincingly at another of Lisa's gentle dabs.

"Not only that," I continued, "but we've wasted a half hour after supper watching you get treated by Florence Nightingale."

"Barely fifteen minutes. Ouch. And I can't help it if chewing food tore open these slashes."

Slashes. Funny that they didn't seem to bother him until Lisa was around.

"And you, Ricky, could—ouch—have a little more patience. It was your brother I rescued from Hezekiah."

"I thought you didn't want to talk about it," I reminded him.

"A person has a duty to let his nurse hear about the injury."

"Then let's get it straight. Joel was playing with Hezekiah so you thought it was safe to scratch the cat behind the ears."

"I don't want to—ouch—talk about it."

I felt better when Lisa winked at me as she dabbed the face cloth.

Ralphy stuck his hand up for quiet. "Company," he announced.

We were in the lower-floor family room. Joel was at the far end, watching television.

Mike gave Ralphy a dirty look as Lisa stood, and he said, "I didn't hear—"

Carl walked through the entrance, followed by a slightly taller man, middle-aged and wearing a neatly pressed gray suit. His tie was a discreet shade of red. He smiled, showing even, white teeth in a lightly tanned, round face. His short hair was thinning, but well groomed.

"I'd like to introduce to you the historian I mentioned last night," Carl said. "He has just arrived after a two-day drive here from Dallas. He'll be helping me with more research on the Gentleman Pirate for my upcoming screenplay."

The rest of us stood beside Lisa to receive the introduction. Joel joined us.

At last, I thought, *someone normal-looking around.* After meeting Doreen, I had almost been ready to believe that most grown-ups around here didn't grow up.

Carl spoke warmly as he pointed to each of us in turn. "Mike, Ricky, Lisa, Joel, Ralphy. And this, I'm pleased to tell you, is Derek Manford, that is, Dr. Derek Manford, professor and Ph.D. in history. Specializing in what's known as . . ."

Dr. Manford smiled. "I wish I had a fancy name for it, Carl. I specialize in the history of the wild west outlaws. And the Gentleman Pirate, of course, was among the best. Or worst." He paused. "And please, let's not get hung up on the doctor part. The title is a silly thing about getting the Ph.D. that mostly just embarrasses me."

What a relief. He spoke in a normal, pleasant voice. He used words we could understand. He was nice and courteous. I was glad to be around someone who didn't have any traces of craziness.

Suddenly, he held his nose and wailed. "A cad! A cad! I dod you said you had no cads!"

With that, Dr. Manford ran out of the room.

Wonderful.

* * * * * * * *

We found him in the kitchen just as he finished his last sneezing fit.

"I'm so sorry," he said, wiping his nose with a pressed handkerchief. "It's just that I'm terribly allergic to cats. There must have been one in the room back there." He stopped, a puzzled look on his face. "But I'm so terribly allergic I would have then been sneezing from the moment I walked into the house."

Carl quickly said, "I can assure you, I don't have a cat."

Dr. Manford put the tip of his forefinger to his nose and thought carefully. "Of course. I suspect it was cat hair imbedded in someone's clothing." He looked at us and said kindly, "All it would take is for one of you to have handled a cat, but that obviously is not true, because my sinuses are fine now."

Before I could explain the culprit, Joel wandered into the kitchen, trailing behind him his teddy bear.

"Well, sir," I began. "Joel here—"

"Aaaaachoooo! Aaaaaachoooo!" Dr. Manford frantically waved his arms for Joel to move away.

"—is going right upstairs to change his clothes," I finished.

"Dan jue. Aaaaaachoooo! Dan jue."

"I beg your pardon, sir?"

"He's trying to say thank you," Carl said with that amused quirk twitching around his mouth.

I took Joel by the hand, led him to our second-floor bedroom, and presented him a clean pair of blue jeans and another T-shirt.

"Try these on before the professor sneezes to death."

Joel changed quickly without saying a word. I grabbed the clothes he had dropped in a pile at his feet. "These go straight to the laundry bin, pal."

His eyes widened and he shook his head.

"Why not?"

Joel quickly stuck his hands in his pockets and pointed with his elbow at the jeans I was holding.

"Don't talk my ears off, pal. Let me guess. There's something in the pockets you don't want washed."

He shrugged and wandered out of the bedroom.

I wasn't sure I wanted to check the pockets. Joel being Joel, there could be anything in there, from a dead frog to a live frog quickly becoming dead.

I turned the pants upside down and shook hard. Two silver dollars thunked the floor. One from each pocket.

Except they weren't silver dollars I'd ever seen before.

I picked them up to look closer. Then my heart started skipping. Whatever they were, they were old. Very old. As in pirate's treasure old.

"Dr. Manford!" I shouted. "Dr. Manford!"

I didn't even realize I was running until I slipped on the bottom step of the stairs and skidded, flat on my back, feet first down the hallway.

"Dr. Manford," I managed to say weakly to all the faces looking down on me. "I have something you might want to see."

The rock we chose on the beach below the cliffs was flat and smooth, and wide enough for all five of us to use for a lunch table. It was also one of the few shelves of rock down by the beach relatively clean of the whitewash marks left behind by target-bombing sea gulls.

"Great idea for Carl to suggest a picnic lunch down here," Lisa said brightly. She tossed her hair back in the sunshine.

If it was the real reason behind the suggestion. Maybe Carl wanted us out of sight to begin searching for the source of Joel's pirate coins. Or maybe he had other arrangements to make.

But I nodded. Even though it was already our third day here, Mike and Ralphy and I had not said anything to Lisa, not wanting to spoil her holiday unless we had very positive proof.

Above our heads, a towering needle of rock cropped out from the side of the cliff. You could almost feel its presence without looking up.

"Close your eyes, Joel, and fold your hands so Lisa can pray."

We all bowed our heads.

Suddenly, a tremendous flapping buffeted my ears, followed by a loud scrambling on the surface of the rock! Then a second buffeting blow of air and another scrambling.

We'd been taught for so long to remain reverent during prayer, that I gritted my teeth and kept my eyes closed. But, I'm sorry to admit, it didn't keep me from wanting Lisa to finish in mid-sentence.

She couldn't resist the urge either and she began racing through the words. When the screeching two feet in front of my face nearly tore out my eardrums, I couldn't help myself. I peeked, ready for a ferocious battle with the noisemaker. With open eyes, I corrected myself. Noisemakers. By then, it was too late. Two sandwiches had been plucked neatly from the tray.

"Amen," Lisa concluded breathlessly a split-second later. By that time, all we saw were scrawny dangling legs five feet in the air and gaining height.

"Thieving banana heads!" Mike was on his feet and shouting with raised fists at the escaping sea gulls.

Ralphy said, "I doubt they consider 'banana head' a real insult, Mike."

I just stared, fascinated. From nowhere, other sea gulls appeared and began divebombing the two carrying our sandwiches. I saw immediately a fact of life for sea gull diners. It's impossible to eat while flying.

To save himself, the first one merely dropped his load.

Mike moaned as it fell. "Roast beef and swiss cheese."

Almost as the sandwich hit the beach, another gull landed, scooped it, tilted its head back and slammed down the entire piece, and hopped into the air again.

The second thief turned, ducked back through the flock like a halfback dodging tackles, skidded to a halt on the beach, and managed to swallow a big chunk before another gull swooped by and tore the remaining piece from him and headed for clear water.

I laughed. "That show was worth losing a couple of sandwiches. By the competition out there, I can see why those first two gulls air raided us like they did."

"Joel's worse," Ralphy said mournfully.

"What?" I turned my head back to the picnic. Joel was already backing away. His cheeks were bulging, and he had a sandwich in each hand.

"Another banana head. This one I can catch . . . " Mike started to move toward Joel.

Lisa gripped his arm. "Be nice, Mike. Remember? He still hasn't told us where he found those coins."

"Besides," I added, "six-year-old kids don't generally care where their hands have been. And he's got a firm grip on that bread."

Unconcerned by any insults, Joel happily watched us from a safe distance and continued eating. He was too smart for us by far. Joel can be just like an aggravating girl. It takes you wanting something for him to decide it's valuable. If I could have kept my head the night before, and casually waited until morning to ask him where he got the dumb coins, he probably would have said something.

But no, my screaming and the stairwell sprint, and all the fussing that followed when Dr. Manford pronounced the coins genuine, only served to convince Joel he had a good secret. Even if he didn't understand what the secret meant. Like aggravating girls, he realized the more someone wants to know a secret, the more fun it is to keep.

So all morning we had spoken to him in sweet tones. Offered him candy. Then helped him down the cliff. Which I realized — as we sat there and smiled phony smiles at him — was only convincing him that the longer he kept the secret, the nicer we would be.

"Three sandwiches left," Mike said. "And four people."

I ducked. "More sea gulls!"

When Mike looked up again after the false alarm, I had all three sandwiches in my hand. "One for you, Lisa. One for you, Ralphy. And one for me." I took a bite, then spoke with my mouth full. "By the way, I don't think this be-nice-to-Joel campaign is too smart."

"Hey!" Mike yelped as Lisa and Ralphy began their sandwiches. "What about me?"

"Mike," I said with as much concern and sympathy as possible, "I'm worried about your poor cheek. Just last night you tore open those huge slashes while you were chewing supper. I'd hate to see it happen again. Good food, huh, Ralphy?"

Ralphy nodded.

That left Mike struggling for words.

Lisa spoke around her smile. "Why shouldn't we work on being nice to Joel?"

"The world's full of banana heads," Mike muttered to himself.

"Think of it," I whispered to her. "Joel's not dumb. He knows once he tells us where he found the coins, we'll have no reason to give him more special treatment."

I paused to close my eyes and savor the food. "Nothing like the ocean air to bring out the taste of food, I always say." With Mike's face twitching satisfactorily, I continued. "So, we need a switch of plans. Something that has a nice ring of poetic justice to it. I suggest that we follow Joel for a change."

I sighed, contemplating the joy of finally outsmarting Joel. Oh, it was turning out to be a sweet afternoon. And nice, too, watching Mike's eyes hungrily follow the last quarter of the sandwich in my hand.

Then, to drive him completely nuts, I threw it as high as possible into the air. Mike ran underneath it to wait, but a sea gull snatched it before it even started falling.

"Just closing the gap," I said to Mike's gasp of disbelief. "When it comes to tricks, I'm now behind you only by a couple hundred."

He looked at me, stunned, then he started laughing.

I was pulling out the wrapped sandwich I had snuck in the back of my shirt while Carl was making lunch. With a bow and flourish, I gave it to Mike.

Friends are great to have.

Since it was my idea, I got elected. Which is why I was trembling under a hedge close to Doreen's house, worried about a cat named Hezekiah and fifty-one of his friends, with Joel less than fifteen feet away and peering into a basement window of Doreen's grand old house.

Joel's concept of privacy doesn't exactly reach society's standards. Like, if it moves, follow it. If the curtains are open, stare inside.

I wondered what was keeping his attention for so long. The house was as big as Carl's and had the same type of exterior. The yard, which like Carl's extended back to the edge of the cliffs, was equally huge and dotted with bushes and the palm trees that make Southern California seem so cool. In fact, one of the few main differences was that Doreen's house had an old stone-walled shed back near the cliffs, and Carl's didn't.

But I wasn't scrunched and hidden to make a report for *Better Homes & Gardens,* even though the house was majestic enough for that magazine's front cover. I was torturing myself simply to find pirate's treasure.

Get out of there, Joel, I shouted at him mentally. *Don't let Doreen catch you. She'll use your skin for a doormat. Go find some more pirate treasure so I can see where you got it from.*

It took a tiny lizard to get Joel away from the window. It flicked its way along the wall in front of him. Joel jumped slightly, then began to stalk it as it continued moving away. By the time the lizard disappeared, Joel had spotted something at the base of a nearby palm tree to grab his attention. After that, it was something else around the side of the house.

A guy could exhaust himself just watching Joel's route, I thought. As soon as he was out of sight, I hauled myself out from under the bush and began tiptoeing to the corner of the house.

On my way by, I couldn't resist peeking in the basement window. I knelt down. Even before I looked inside, the waft of cat smell blasted my face. Then I saw why.

The basement floor seemed to be covered with hundreds of them. Lying down, stretching, sniffing corners, pouncing on imaginary mice. My eyes grew accustomed enough to the dim light in the basement to see that the cats had total freedom. Almost beneath me, a custom-built cat stairway ran from the basement to the first floor. It was narrow and led to a small open doorway at the top. Cats calmly moved up and down. Others were relaxed and sprawled on various steps.

In short, cat heaven. But a cleaning woman's nightmare. The smell was strong, even to me in the fresh air on the outside. I didn't want to guess at how badly it smelled inside. No wonder Doreen had bags and bags of cat litter to bury.

I gave my head a shake. Doreen! What was I doing daydreaming in her territory? I glanced around to make sure I was still safe, then I ran, crouched, to the corner of the house to check on Joel's progress.

I froze.

Joel was in the middle of the lawn, far from the nearest bush or tree. He was on his knees, staring intently at some blades of grass. Bugs fascinated him, especially ugly ones.

What froze me was the size of the cat stalking him. Hezekiah! The gray cat was squat and solid like a small bulldog. One ear missing and only a stub remaining for a tail. A cat that was no stranger to fights. And it was slinking along the ground, intent on Joel's back.

Should I shout? Risk Doreen hearing me? Put Joel on guard for the rest of the day and ensure we would not find his source of pirate coins?

Hezekiah decided for me. Before I could decide, he broke into a run and leaped for Joel's back.

They tumbled to the ground. As I took a step to rescue Joel, I heard the laughter of delight. Joel came up with a grin, holding Hezekiah in both arms.

Of course, I reminded myself. Mike had caught them playing yesterday. Fortunately, I wasn't going to be as dumb as Mike to think Hezekiah was as innocent as he appeared in Joel's arms. I've seen enough of my brother to know that he can tame anything. Like the time he brought two mice into church and I ended up losing them. Or the way the most terrifying dogs in Jamesville wag their tails when he walks by.

No sir, Mike was welcome to the slashes on his cheek. Joel was welcome to Hezekiah. Hezekiah was welcome to as much distance from me as he wanted.

Joel scratched behind Hezekiah's ears. It was such a big cat that the purring sounded like distant rumbling thunder.

Get on with it, Joel. Be our human metal detector and find some more coins.

Joel giggled at something he whispered into Hezekiah's ear. They started walking away from me. I groaned. *Not the shed, Joel.*

Naturally, he didn't listen to my impassioned mental plea. Not only did he walk directly to the shed, he picked up Hezekiah, draped him over his shoulder, and opened the door to slip inside.

Wonderful.

If I wanted to spy on them, I had miles and miles of open lawn to cover. Joel could walk out anytime. Doreen could appear anytime. I began to think it would be easier to be a mouse trying to bell a cat.

On the other hand, maybe at this moment, Joel was thinking

about making another stop on his route, a stop for more coins.
Or maybe the coins were inside.

I sighed, pushed myself away from the wall, and bolted across
the lawn. I simply had to reach the side of the shed before Joel
wandered out again.

I made it within seconds, and leaned against the shed while
my heart came back down to earth. Then a movement caught the
corner of my eye. And my heart hammered its way back into
orbit.

Doreen. I was caught between the frying pan and the fire.

Her back was to me as she was letting herself through the
fence gate, barely a throwing distance away.

I chose the frying pan inside the shed, away from Doreen. I'd
sort it out with Joel and Hezekiah later. If I survived.

As Doreen fumbled with the gate catch, I slipped inside the
shed and braced myself for a hurtling cat attack.

"Don't panic, Joel. It's only me," I hissed into the semi-dark-
ness. "And whatever you do, don't let go of that vicious cat."

He didn't reply. But my face was still safe.

I decided to let myself breathe as I took stock of the situation.
The light was murky because of the dirt on the tiny window that
filtered out the sunlight. Heavy beams ran across the ceiling
above me. The stone walls were rough. Scattered garden tools
and busted-up lawn furniture cluttered the floor. In one corner
lay a pile of burlap potato sacks, like the one Doreen had been
emptying on the cliff.

Then I thought I was losing my mind. Joel was nowhere to be
seen.

"Joel," I hissed louder. "Joel! Stop hiding."

Nothing.

This is not happening, I told myself. *Not even Joel can disappear in such a ghostly fashion.*

I pulled myself together. *Reenact his movements,* I thought.
He comes inside. He's curious. He's stands right where I am

standing to look around. Maybe hears the noise outside of my feet running. Keeps the cat draped around his neck. Walks to the window.

I walked to the window.

Hmm. He's shorter. Can't quite see outside. Pulls himself up—bingo! I saw the smudged prints of tiny fingers on the sill.

OK. He needs to step up for a better look. He decides to step up onto this little stone ledge, the one runing around the base of the shed. Then what?

I looked closer. One of the stones of the ledge under the window seemed out of line.

I placed my foot on it and pushed to see if it was loose. The world went black and crazy.

I'm sure that only an instant passed. But time seemed to swirl. My mind stepped aside and noted with objective satisfaction: *Ricky, you're falling, it'll probably hurt when you land, and you'd better land soon or you'll be in big trouble.*

My body answered my smug mind by thumping something solid.

"Ooof."

Mind and body joined and both told me my backside was going to be throbbing for a couple of days.

It was pitch black. My hands felt beneath me. Rough packed dirt.

Wonderful.

Then a banshee yowling filled my universe.

I think I managed a whimper before something hard, round, and solid butted my breath away. And while I was sucking desperately for air, something wild, frantic, and full of razor blades landed on my head.

10

•

"I don't want—ouch—want to talk about it, Mike. Not even for a second."

"Yes, you do. I could tell by the twitchy look around your eyes as you explained it to Carl and Dr. Manford. There's more to the story than you let on at supper."

"Yeah," Ralphy chimed in, "and a simple collision, as you put it, with Joel and the guard cat might explain your face but doesn't tell us why your hands are scraped up."

"Or," Lisa added quietly as she dabbed a warm damp washcloth against one of my deeper scratches, "why you had that red dirt ground into your blue jeans."

I put up my hands helplessly. "OK, OK. What are you guys? Detectives? I did have more to tell. But I wanted to make sure nobody else was around."

We were sitting in lawn chairs at the back of Carl's yard. The cool air had a magic stillness as the darkness of early evening dropped upon us. Diamond points of brightness. The muted crying of night insects. The wash of waves far below us.

For a moment, I forgot myself, the scratches on my face, the staggering news I had for my friends. The California moment was proving something Dad had tried teaching me once. "It's God's world, son," he had said, "just slow down enough to listen and feel and hear and see all at once, without thinking about all the things that you let clutter your life, and then you'll know what beauty is."

Mike, always impatient, said, "Get to it, pal. There's still half an hour on the dryer cycle."

"Thanks, Mike." Of course, Dad had not counted on red-headed friends interrupting your contemplation.

I focused my mind on the story I was about to tell, grateful that there was indeed half an hour left on the dryer cycle. It was an old trick to keep Joel out of our way. Toss his teddy bear in the dryer and he'll sit there, unmoving, until the cycle ends and he can finally rescue it.

"First of all," I said, "I think I found a pirate's tunnel."

Lisa nearly jabbed my eye in surprise.

"But," I continued despite the sudden pain added to all my other little ones, "I didn't want to tell Carl or Dr. Manford, for a couple of reasons." One being I didn't completely trust Carl, but I couldn't let Lisa know that. "It would've been embarrassing to explain the fact that I was on Doreen's property. Also, I thought it would be a nice surprise if we tracked down the treasure ourselves, and then told them about the tunnel."

I paused, savoring the moment. The three of them hung on every word.

"Get on with it, pal!" Mike blurted.

"Yeah," Ralphy said. "When, where, how."

Lisa simply regarded me calmly under the brightening moonlight.

"Well," I began slowly. I told them all of it, from the beginning where Joel had been spying through the basement window that leaked out the smell of a zoo.

Then I explained the stone-walled shed.

"Joel must have found the loose coins somewhere in there. And that's why I'm convinced the tunnel belonged to pirates. You know how Joel's got that sense for finding things. Those coins probably dropped once when they were moving their treasure and it took Joel to find them in a dusty corner."

There was a moment of respectful silence as we all visualized

Joel's unstoppable curiosity and the way he must have stumbled across the coins.

"The stone underneath the window triggered a release on a trapdoor," I continued. "One that springs back shut automatically. I went back later when Joel was returning Hezekiah. It's virtually impossible to spot any seams on the floor."

Mike was nearly squirming. "Forget the shed. Forget the trapdoor. Just tell us about the tunnel!"

I shrugged. "There wasn't much to see. It was dark."

"Aaaaaaagh!" Mike jumped up and shot his hands around my neck.

"However," I said thoughtfully in response to the pressure on my throat, "once I convinced Joel that the person dropping in was his loving older brother, I did have a chance to explore it anyway."

"That's better," Mike grumbled. He returned to his sitting position.

"Let me get this straight," Lisa said. The only bad part about my story was that it interested her so much she had forgotten about the tender care of my face. "You're in the shed. You drop through a trapdoor, survive a head butt from a brother who doesn't know it's you, and a cat attack, and then find out you can't open the trapdoor to get out again."

"Exactly. But Hezekiah and Joel did such a good job terrifying me, I didn't have time to get scared about anything else. Like being trapped there forever."

"Or," from Ralphy, "since you didn't run into skeletons, you knew the pirate hadn't used it as a place to get rid of people."

"That too. Plus something else. I think I dropped about five feet. And it didn't make sense that someone would build a tunnel with such an inconvenient way to get down. Then, in the dark, I smacked my head into some stone stairs. The stone stairs that would have saved me the drop in the first place. That's when I decided the tunnel must lead somewhere. So I crawled along, feeling my way, and found out that—" I paused triumphantly, even as I shivered to remember how scary it was blindly groping in the cool mustiness of the pitch black tunnel—"it did lead somewhere. To a door much farther along the tunnel."

"What was on the other side?" Mike never could let a guy tell a story the way he wanted.

"I couldn't open it."

Mike groaned. Served him right.

I drew a breath remembering how long I had stood forlornly in absolute dark with Joel and his cat at my side. Remembering how it had helped just being able to pray. "But I knew that door was my only way out. And that's how I scraped my hands. I pushed and pulled on everything I could find jutting out of the walls around it. And finally, I triggered another release."

"I can't stand this," Mike moaned.

"On the other side of the door was . . ." Lisa coached me.

"Bright sunshine and the side of the cliff. The door was cleverly concealed behind a huge boulder. And when I stepped around the boulder, I was at the base of that huge outcrop we could see from the beach, the rock that looked like a needle-shaped tower."

"Did you find any treasure?" Ralphy asked.

"Didn't look," I stated. "Thought I would save the search for all of us to do together. I mean, what are friends for?"

What I wasn't going to tell them was that I had been so grateful to be out of that dark tomb and in warm California sunshine that I had cried, and that I had been so happy to be alive the last thing on my mind had been pirate's treasure.

"What a pal," Mike said happily. "So tomorrow, then, we can search for it."

"B-but what if Doreen catches us in her shed?" Sometimes I thought the only difference between Ralphy and me was that he actually showed his fears.

Lisa snapped her fingers. "Maybe we won't have to use the

shed. Think, guys. If it was a secret tunnel for pirates, don't you figure they would have a way to open that cliff door from the outside?"

"Of course!" Ralphy cried. "We'll be safe on the cliff. We can take some flashlights to explore the whole tunnel in peace."

If only he had been completely right.

But like the thickheaded person I am, I let his sense of security lull me. "It'll be great, guys. We'll be rich."

Before we could speculate further, Joel wandered toward us with a resentful look in his eye and a teddy bear in his hand.

I stood. "Probably bedtime for that twerp. Why don't we head into the house."

I put Joel to bed, then enjoyed the next few hours playing Monopoly with the gang. Mike, who insisted it was no trouble to be the banker, had this habit of providing himself interest-free loans, but we cured him by voting to seize his property.

Later, when everyone was asleep, I almost wish that I had stayed in bed, instead of slipping back downstairs for a drink of juice.

Carl was on the living room phone and his voice was far too easy to overhear as he spoke softly.

"No problem, man. The kids are all asleep. Slip by in an hour. I'll be waiting out front."

Silence.

Then, "Just cut your motor as you approach. When you're ready to go, I'll push your car down the street and you can start it there. They won't wake up. I promise."

I decided that opening the fridge door might not be too smart. Orange juice could wait until morning. And being a moderate chicken, I wanted to be alive and well in the morning to be able to drink it then.

11

Our fourth morning in California, and we were ready to start painting Carl's master bedroom. True to his schedule of morning work and afternoon play, we had already finished two other rooms, like this: Cover the floors with plastic. Sand the walls. Fill holes and cracks with putty. Resand. Brush on a coat of primer. Sand lightly. Then apply one coat of FAUN BEIGE LATEX SPREADS EASILY DRIES QUICKLY CLEANS WITH NO FUSS. Sand lightly one final time and then paint on the second and last coat of faun beige latex.

Dr. Manford, whose room was on the third floor, stayed out of the way most of the time during our painting sessions. I wasn't quite sure how he officially researched things, but he seemed to divide his time between the library and the cliffs.

"I can't believe it," Mike groaned as he clicked on our paint-splattered portable radio. "Look at all that sanding Ricky has to do."

I nodded.

Lisa placed her hand lightly on my elbow. "Are you OK, pal?"

I nodded again and continued my staring at the far wall.

"It's just that you seem preoccupied," she whispered, "and you just let Mike get away with giving you a rotten sanding job." She pointed at the ceiling.

I snapped out of my daze. It was no time to explain to Lisa I had been wondering about her uncle's midnight rendezvous barely nine hours earlier. I would tell Mike and Ralphy about it later;

not that there was much to tell. A dark car had coasted up to the front of the house. Carl had hurried out, given something to the driver, taken something back, and pushed the car down the street. From my vantage point at a second-story window, I had seen little else. At breakfast, Carl had been his usual smiling self.

My eyes followed Lisa's pointing finger. Defects in the ceiling panels had left three grooved lines—one long, two short—in slow random squiggles. A few more were etched in the far corner.

"Sure I'll sand, Mike. As long as you hold the ladder and get me water when I need it."

"Water?"

"Yup. Sanding's dusty and thirsty work."

It took two glassfuls spilled on his head to convince him the system wouldn't work.

"I've got an idea," he then suggested. "Those grooves look too deep. We should leave the ceiling for last. Maybe Carl knows a better way."

"Why didn't I think of that?" I said as I moved down the ladder, stepping only once on Mike's fingers.

The rest of the morning went quickly. Our discussions covered what we would buy with the riches we were about to find in the tunnel that afternoon.

Except we found nothing.

Sure, we found the door, half hidden by brush behind the boulder. Sure, we found a way to get inside the tunnel, by a simple twisting of an odd-shaped rock immediately above and to the left of the old wooden door. Sure, we wandered up and down the six-foot-high passageway with our flashlights. And sure, we even found a way to open the shed's trapdoor from the inside, by pushing a lever at the top of the gray-white stone stairs.

But no treasure.

The floor along the entire tunnel was packed hard dirt, a reddish clay almost as solid as concrete. The walls and ceiling of the tunnel were shored with beams of lumber, but gave no clues or hints of a massive buried treasure.

"Nuts!" Mike muttered on the side of the cliff as we shut the door behind us after two hours of fruitless searching. "A pirate's tunnel and no stupid treasure."

The rest of us gathered behind him at the base of the towering needle-shaped rock. It jutted away from the cliff at an angle much too steep to climb, if one was crazy enough to contemplate such a thing.

We moved reluctantly along a path away from the rock tower. Below us and across the water, we could see the Pirate's Haven.

Mike picked up a rock and threw it far into the open space between us and the ocean below.

"Eat that, you dumb sea gulls," he muttered.

His lousy mood carried to the rest of us. It was a letdown, all of us dreaming about video games and new skateboards and bikes and cameras only to discover nothing.

We were silent until we reached the top of the cliff.

"Wonderful," I said with a sniff. "On top of all of that, we have to put up with the smell of the cat lady's house."

The zoo smell that had made my eyes water as I looked in the basement window the day before was now strong in the air. All of us gagged briefly and made sour faces.

Then Ralphy spoke as we began trudging back across Carl's wide backyard. "I was just thinking," he said.

"That's dangerous," Mike noted.

Ralphy ignored him and began counting off his fingers as he spoke. "We can conclude three possibilities. One, the treasure was there and we couldn't find it. But we searched completely, so we can rule that out. Or two, the treasure was there at one point, but someone already found it. Unlikely, or we'd have heard about it. Or three, the treasure was never there."

"But why go through all that trouble to build such a secret tunnel?" I protested.

"That's the whole point. Why?"

Lisa's eyes brightened. "Because you're a pirate who wants to move from one place to another without being seen."

"Exactly," Ralphy nodded. "Our next task is to start looking for clues in the opposite direction."

"Huh?" Mike said.

"Opposite," I coached. "It means in the other direction. Away from. That kind of thing. Ralphy's trying to tell us we need to start searching on the outside of the tunnel. Not on the inside."

I looked to Ralphy to see if he was agreeing.

His attention was elsewhere.

"Right, Ralphy?"

He turned his head back to us.

"Did any of you see that?" he asked.

"The boy's losing his head," Mike warned.

"See what?" Lisa asked.

"Flashes of light from Doreen's house. From up near the attic windows."

We all stared, but saw nothing.

"Sorry," Ralphy said. "Probably sun bouncing off the ocean against the glass."

"Like I said. Losing his head." Mike stopped and brightened. "Hey, I'm a poet. And I just showed it."

"Forget poetry," Lisa laughed. "You'd make a better living from finding buried treasure."

Mike snorted. "The treasure's long gone."

Lisa smiled. "I rest my case."

12

On your day off of painting, it's not much fun waking up to comb your hair in the mirror after a cat as unscrupulous as Hezekiah has played patty-cake with your face. Despite the fact that two days had passed since falling into the pirate's tunnel, I still looked worse than a misplaced Indian warrior.

In other words, my looks made it easier to decline a Saturday morning trip to the beach. "I'd like to go to the library instead," I informed everyone at the breakfast table.

Hoots greeted me. Carl smiled his quirky smile at the hoots. Dr. Manford, in crisply ironed dress pants and a short-sleeved shirt, continued his staring out the window. Joel chose that moment to begin his disappearing act. He made the mistake of brushing my knee as he tried sneaking past me under the table.

"Research," I defended myself. My voice came out as a grunt because of the effort it took to hold Joel by his beltloop. "Pirate research. I thought I'd read as much as I could on the subject. Maybe I'll be lucky enough to find one of Dr. Manford's books."

At that, Dr. Manford swung his attention back to the table. "The one you'd need is called *California Outlaws: A History of Daring.* I'd love to offer you a personal copy, Ricky. But unfortunately, my own library, of course, is back home."

Joel gave up tugging underneath the table and sat at my feet.

"Then I guess it's the library for me. Other, less civilized people would obviously prefer to burn their skin and sit in hot, sticky sand."

More hoots. Not that I wanted them to know my own prefer-ence was hot, sticky sand. I thought of how fun it would be to skateboard to the public beach on the steep road that wound from these houses high in La Jolla down to the public beach. But something told me we needed more background on the Gentle-man Pirate if we wanted to find his long-buried treasure.

Carl asked, "Will you be taking Joel to the bea—." He stopped to look for him, puzzled. "How does that kid do it?"

"He's under the table, sir. It just happens."

Carl stroked his goatee thoughtfully. "Could one of you do me a favor and stay close to the house today? With Joel. I'd hate to see him get lost at the beach."

Ralphy volunteered. He wasn't fond, anyway, of blinding peo-ple with his skinny white chest.

"Great," Carl said. "You guys have been doing good work. I'll do the breakfast dishes so you can scatter."

He seemed like such a nice guy, I felt guilty for questioning his motives. *Why did he want to be by himself?*

Before I could decide if I should hang around to spy—unno-ticed, of course—Dr. Manford made my decision for me. "Ricky," he observed, "Mike and Lisa look like they're raring to leave. Any chance you can do me a small favor? I was down at the ocean yesterday and I misplaced my sunglasses. If you could go down the cliffs and take a quick look around, I'd appreciate it. I have an appointment right away."

I nodded without thinking. Dr. Manford was so pleasant all the time, you never minded helping him.

That was it for breakfast. Except for one thing. When I tried walking away from the table, I fell flat on my face.

Joel had tied my shoelaces together.

* * * * * * * *

California Outlaws: A History of Daring was a large brown hard-cover book. It was easy to find in the local history section of the library. Unfortunately, the information in it on the Gentleman Pirate was sketchy; it covered less than half a page of the chapter on Southern California outlaws. There was little more there than what Carl had told us upon our arrival.

However, there's always more than one way to find something out in a library. I left the book open and face down on my table to mark the pages. Then I went back to the card catalog.

When I returned to my table with three other history books, I discovered I had a visitor. A ladybug.

It had crawled along Dr. Manford's book and then gotten stuck on a tape mark near the bottom right corner of the cover. Seeing it reminded me of Joel, and I smiled. Joel would stare at the bug for minutes, I was sure, then carefully work its legs free and gently set it free. So I looked around to make sure nobody was watching, and did the same.

"You and your family owe me a big one, pal," I growled at the ladybug as it flexed its wings. It ignored me and whirred across through the bright sunshine that shone into the library.

Then I realized what I'd done and sighed deeply enough to earn a cross look from the librarian. I couldn't even shake Joel's presence when he was gone. Good thing Mike hadn't seen me talking to bugs.

I resumed concentration on the books. I found a discouraging article, though I photocopied it for Mike, Ralphy and Lisa anyway. It came from an exciting book on San Diego's history.

The Gentleman Pirate used his unique escape method along the California coastline for twenty years despite the fact that he knew very little about sailing. In fact, it was only through the skill of his trusted friend and navigational partner, Joseph Dominga, that the Gentleman Pirate was able to be a pirate at all.

Each outlaw foray involved the same method. Dominga would pilot the ship close to shore, then anchor it. The

Gentleman Pirate and his band would ferry horses ashore on low flatboats and complete the raid while Dominga waited onboard the ship for their return.

Ironically, toward the end, their very success drove them apart. The wealth they accumulated was so great that the Gentleman Pirate began to fear Captain Dominga would betray him and cast him adrift while out at sea. So Dominga's daughter was held hostage on land until the Gentleman Pirate's safe return to the "Pirate's Haven" at the end of each voyage.

Their partnership proved that there is no honor among thieves, as the Gentleman Pirate eventually caught Dominga stealing from their booty. For the sake of old friendship, the Gentleman Pirate only banished Dominga from the "Haven," instead of seeking the customary execution.

Dominga was murdered shortly after by bandits who were seeking his half of a treasure map it was rumored he and the Gentleman Pirate had once made. No treasure map was found in his possession.

The Gentleman Pirate did not make any more raids and died of pneumonia six months later; no trace of his alleged half of the map was found among his belongings either. With both of them dead, an incalculable amount of coin and jewelry was lost forever, probably anywhere among the hundreds of miles of coastline that they had frequented.

The "Pirate's Haven" has since lapsed into obscurity, and is only a curiosity point along the La Jolla cliffs for diligent historians.

And historians, I told myself, at least find value in history instead of treasures. Unlike other searchers who wanted actual treasure. Mike and Ralphy could start in one direction and Lisa and I could start in the other. With the four of us, it would only

take a couple of centuries to dig up all of the California coastline. And the treasure had probably been swept away by a storm
anyway. Who were we to kid ourselves that we could find a
treasure when the people who knew the most about it, historians,
were smart enough not to bother.

Sitting there, I preferred it when I had believed we were close
to something, when I could rescue ladybugs because I was in a
good mood.

I returned to Carl's house. Ralphy and Joel were not in sight
and the house was empty. Just as well. I wasn't in a hurry to
break bad news to my friends.

I went to the kitchen, absently peeled a banana, and threw the
peels in the garbage can attached to the cupboard door underneath the sink. One part of my mind noted a handful of small
stiff cardboard backings scattered on top of the garbage. Before I
could wonder about it, the kitchen door slammed open.

Mike looked around, then moved forward to stand beside me.
"Boy, I'm glad you're here," he said in a low tone as he fought to
breathe evenly.

"I missed you too," I said.

He didn't catch the sarcasm in my voice. I should have known
then something was up. Instead, the playing-card-sized pieces of
cardboard were bothering me.

"What do you make of this?" I asked, pointing into the garbage
can.

He closed the cupboard door without looking. "Forget that," he
said unevenly. I realized he had just finished running hard. "Lisa
may be in trouble."

I caught the pleading urgency that finally escaped through his
voice, and the skin at the back of my neck crawled. It wasn't
often that Mike showed fear so plainly.

"The man at the beach," Mike continued, no longer bothering
to control his heaving lungs. "The guy with the eyepatch who
made the first deal with Carl. I think he's kidnapped Lisa."

My reply to Mike's hoarse words had been a hurried dash for my skateboard.

Among hopped curbs, dodged parked cars, and startled pedestrians, Mike explained the story as we zinged down the road that wound down to the public beach. It wasn't until we reached the boardwalk that I realized how dangerously crazy that skateboard run had been. Without fear to keep us in motion, there was no way we would have survived it, even going half as fast.

As Mike explained, he had left Lisa alone at their towels on the beach to buy a couple of Cokes. On his return, he had spotted and recognized the man Carl had given money to on our first day in California. Which would have been OK, but he was squatting in the sand, actually talking to Lisa.

Unwilling to lose his advantage of surprise, Mike squatted behind a bench and simply watched. The man had stood, then reached down and pulled Lisa up by the hand. Lisa had followed him without protesting.

Leaving his Cokes in the sand, Mike had done the only thing he thought safe. He followed them, right to the restaurant Carl had entered with his bag of money only four days earlier. Lisa and the patch-man had walked inside without looking back.

Mike had waited, nervously, for fifteen minutes, then worked up the courage to slip inside. And found nothing. At that, not quite sure enough of a crime to call the police, he had bolted and skateboarded to Carl's house, hoping to find me or Ralphy.

Our first destination was the restaurant overlooking the boardwalk.

"Play cool, now," Mike cautioned me as we joined the moving crowd of people along the wide wooden boardwalk. "We don't want to look out of the ordinary."

Despite the chill of worry which reduced the blazing sun to a minor distraction, I managed a snort. "So define normal, pal," I said from the corner of my mouth as I scanned the jostling crowds.

He grinned weakly. "Good point."

Call it Southern California. Ahead of us and coming our way, a tiny wrinkled-brown woman old enough to be my grandmother roller-skated in and out of the pedestrian flow. She wore tight purple spandex and pushed herself along with flourescent green ski poles. To our right, and perched on the concrete seawall which divided the boardwalk from the sand, were two girls wrapped in black loose shawls. With matching orange spiked hair and double nose rings jutting from their nostrils, they scowled at my brief stare. There was a hugely fat lady with rolls that bulged out far enough to overlap her skimpy bikini. She oiled herself intently as she waddled down the sidewalk; unwary strollers bounced off her like bumper cars, taking with them smudged marks of grease as souvenirs. There were preening beauty queens, surfer dudes, guitar players, bikers, skateboarders, and a skinny black guy on a unicycle. It was enough to make me think Doreen the cat lady was quite normal, thank you.

But there was no sign of a pretty, dark-haired girl in a modest one-piece bathing suit who preferred to read romances on the beach. Our Lisa.

"Can we hurry, Mike? Let's get to that restaurant and ask questions. Maybe somebody saw them leave."

"I don't think it's a good idea."

"Don't be ridiculous," I said firmly. "Right now, it's the only idea we have."

* * * * * * * *

"Don't be ridiculous, huh?" Mike muttered under his breath. "It's the only idea we have, huh?"

"You didn't tell me it was like this," I protested as quietly as possible. A person tends to not want to make much noise when three hoods with extended switchblades are slowly backing that person into a corner.

Despite the building's age, from the outside the restaurant had not looked sinister. It was called THE BLUE PELICAN—FRE H SEAFOOD, with the *S* obviously long gone by the way the wooden sign was bleached gray from years of facing the ocean and sun. Inside, my skin had immediately prickled warning signals of urgency. As in urgently leave.

Clouds of smoke swirled. It was dimly lit despite the bright afternoon sun outside, and the actual restaurant area inside had been reduced to a cluster of wobbly tables and swaybacked chairs. Most of the rest of the inside was devoted to pool tables under single lightbulbs, scattered card tables, and tough-looking guys with dirty white T-shirts and muscles big enough to carry wide, ugly tattoos. And all of them looking taller than lighthouses.

I had stupidly pressed forward, despite the prickling of my skin that warned me of danger. "Excuse me," I had said politely to one guy leaning on a pool cue. "We're looking for a friend."

He had stared down on us, then had reached into his pocket and pulled a switchblade. He popped open the blade, and casually picked his teeth as he stared. "So?"

"We think she came in here. About my height. Dark hair."

He picked his teeth for a few more seconds before replying. "Naw, kid. We ain't seen no dame like that. Besides, we like them older. Haw. Haw."

I gulped. "Maybe did you see a guy with an eye patch? Describe him, Mike."

Mike glared at me. "He, uh, wore an eye patch. A big guy, with a brushcut and an eye patch."

"Naw. Hey, ain't it time for your afternoon nappies?"

Mike grinned politely.

I squeezed Mike's arm for courage. "We're pretty sure he came in here. About a half hour ago."

"I been here all day. I ain't seen nothing."

Mike spoke again. "But I followed him in here."

Suddenly, the guy stopped picking his teeth. His insolent slouch became a menacing crouch. "You said you were following Big Joe?"

Mike nodded hesitantly.

"Boys," the hood called out. "We got us some snoops."

Two other hoods moved in as Mike and I backed away.

"And you know what we do to snoops?"

We were smart enough not to ask. Instead, we stepped backwards a few more steps.

Click. Click. Two more switchblades appeared.

That's when Mike muttered under his breath, "Don't be ridiculous, huh? It's the only idea we have, huh?"

We suddenly banged into a wall behind us. No place left to run. All three of them blocked our escape in front.

The first hood snarled. "'Round here, nobody messes with Big Joe." *Big Joe! We now knew Patch-Man's name.* The snarling continued. "Because when he don't take care of them, we do. A few nicks on those pretty faces of yours will be a good enough lesson, don't you think?"

Mike said, "Actually, we've always been quick learners and I'm sure the message is quite clear and—"

At the same time, I was saying, "We're working undercover for my dad who's a cop and him and three other cops are outside the restaurant right now and if we're not out in thirty seconds, he'll be coming in here looking to bust heads and—"

The other two hoods laughed.

The first hood rested the point of his switchblade delicately just inside my nostril. "Good try kid. But the story's as old as dinosaurs. I think we'll slit this side first."

Would he actually have done it? I really don't know. Maybe he was just bluffing, hoping to scare us so badly that we'd never come back. But I didn't have a chance to find out.

The door banged open and two cops stepped inside. They were big and burly and a joy to my eyes.

Click. Click. Click. The three switchblades disappeared so quickly I almost wondered if they had really existed.

"Nice day for a convention," the first cop boomed.

The first hood's eyes bulged in surprise.

"Sure is," he finally said, then scowled at me. "We was just talking to your kid about how nice a day it was." He elbowed me. "Right?"

"Right," I said loudly, then quickly walked toward the door, the cops, and safety.

"Our kid?" the first cop was quietly saying to the other cop as we eased our way past them.

At the door, I couldn't resist the urge to stop. Miracle or not, you have to take advantage of some of the coincidences in life. "Thanks, Dad," I called back. "You can take over from here." *Let them sort out the confusion.*

We scooted into bright wonderful sunshine. And blinked in surprise. Lisa was leaning against the seawall across the boardwalk. She smiled strangely.

"Tsk. Tsk. You guys pick such strange places to visit."

"YOU!" Mike and I both croaked.

"Of course me. Who else would have sent those cops in there?"

Wonderful. That's what I like about successful rescue missions. The gratitude you earn from the damsels in distress.

"We thought you were—"

"Happy to be reading on the beach," I interrupted Mike before he could say "kidnapped." Because then we would have to explain to her Carl's paper bag of money and why we thought he was a drug dealer. Yet I, too, desperately wanted to know what had happened, and why she wasn't kidnapped. I asked a safe question instead. "How'd you know we were in there anyway?"

"Like I can't recognize Mike's Hawaiian shirt a mile away? I saw you guys skulking along the boardwalk and decided to follow. Then I peaked inside the restaurant and saw those guys lining you up against the wall. It seemed like a good time to ask help from a couple of cops walking this beat."

It wasn't the explanation I was hoping for. Why wasn't she telling us about the patch-man?

Mike started sputtering. "You spied on us. Of all the—"

"Mike, she saved our hides." As if he hadn't been doing the same to her earlier in the afternoon.

I knew the real problem was this sudden stalemate, a block between friends. We were hiding something from her, which she didn't know. She was suddenly hiding something from us, which we knew, but not why. Who would bring up the subject of the patch-man first?

Before Mike could say anything else, both cops strode out of the restaurant and stopped in front of us. They were middle-aged with greying crewcuts.

They stared at me and Mike calmly. "The punks in there told us you're clean," the first one said. "But everybody knows it's the place for deals. We figure one of two things happened in there."

The second one nodded. "You stumbled into a bad place and said the wrong thing. Or you're part of the drug scene. Today, we'll give you the benefit of the doubt. But if we see you in there again, things'll get rough from our end."

Mike and I could only nod speechlessly.

The cops turned and walked away. The first one's voice carried faintly back. "Can you understand those punks calling us 'Dad' in there? What happened to the good old days when we were 'cops.' Or even 'pigs.' I wish I could keep up on these things."

"You're right, Sam," the second one replied. "It makes me feel old too."

* * * * * * * *

The typewritten note simply read:

Ricky, Mike and Lisa. Have had a short notice opportunity to watch a film shooting in Hollywood. Couldn't find any of you, so I took Ralphy and Joel. We should be back Monday. Hope you can forgive us for not waiting, but it looked too good to pass up the chance.
Carl.

Lisa, who had been reading the note aloud to me and Mike, became very still.

"I think they left about an hour ago," Dr. Manford said. "Because I found it on the kitchen table when I returned from a mid-afternoon stroll."

Lisa nodded without speaking, set the note back down on the table, smiled tightly, and left the kitchen.

"Oh dear," Dr. Manford said, "she didn't seem too happy. If

she feels that bad about missing the trip, I can always drive her there myself. I have a tight research schedule, but some things are more important."

I smiled bravely, despite the knot in my own stomach. "Very nice of you to offer, sir, but she should be OK." I turned to Mike. "We need to oil our skateboard wheels, remember?"

I walked outside quickly, knowing Mike would follow.

We reached the lawn chairs that overlooked the ocean. The sun was an hour from the far horizon. The breeze at the edge of the cliffs and the distant wash of waves should have made it a peaceful moment.

It wasn't.

"This is big trouble, Mike."

I wasn't used to seeing a thoughtful expression on his face. It only confirmed the size of the trouble.

I began. "Lisa is weird right now and it's got to be over Carl, but we don't know what kind of hold he has on her. And by the way she reacted, you can bet that note wasn't telling the truth."

"Which means the note has to be a cover up. But why would Carl take Ralphy and Joel?"

"While we were at the beach, they probably stumbled across something he couldn't afford to let them spread to anyone else," I said. "But we can't prove it."

Mike stood and kicked at a clump of grass. "You're telling me that we have to sit here and wait?"

"Think about it. We can't run around and shout 'kidnapper.' No one would believe us. And there's still the problem of Lisa. What does she know? And why can't she tell?"

Mike stopped halfway through his next kick. His jaw dropped and his freckles seemed to lose color. "No way. No way. No way."

"What!"

"It can't be."

"Mike, I'll pull your tongue out of your head if you don't tell me."

He sat heavily beside me. "I hate to think about it, but it's the only thing that makes sense. Pretend for a second that Lisa knows what Carl does, at least about the drug part."

"And she would," I said heavily. "If she spent time with Big Joe the patch-man this afternoon, and he let her go."

"That's what scares me. She knows about Carl, but he won't hurt her, because she's his niece. So maybe he gets around it by threatening to hurt Ralphy and Joel if she blabs. It's, it's . . ."

"Blackmail," I finished quietly. "It would also explain why she pretended nothing happened this afternoon. Poor Lisa can't say anything to us, or to the police. It must be killing her."

We both stared at the waves below us. Squawking gulls circled the beach, swooping, diving, and fighting among themselves.

Finally I spoke again. "There is some hope." I thought of the stalemate between Lisa and us, and realized there was another one as well. "Lisa might have to keep quiet, but Carl's hold on her is good only as long as Ralphy and Joel are safe."

Mike smiled wanly. "How long will that last?"

"That's the question, isn't it. We'll simply have to find them before Carl changes the formula."

15

They lowered me by rope deep into the catacombs that held the hungry lions. It was a crazy, last-gasp chance, but without it, Joel would have no chance of surviving. I only hoped he was alive, that somehow he had avoided the prowling, raging lions whose roars echoed among the caves.

I hoped I would come out alive too.

As I touched the bone-littered floor, the musky stench of cat in the stifling warm air overwhelmed me. I fought the urge to gag, terrified that any unnecessary noise might attract a lion.

The first tunnel of the catacomb was straight ahead, dark in the flickering of my candle. How would I find Joel among the maze of tunnels. I didn't know, but I had to look.

I moved forward and the smell of cat grew stronger, almost suffocating me.

Then I heard it. A slight dislodging of gravel, the sound of huge padded feet moving closer. Before I could react, the huge beast was there, its eyes twin gleams of anger and hunger. It filled the tunnel in front of me, and with a roar that deafened me, it charged!

I fell back and it was on me. I crashed to the ground in a hurricane tangle of fur and . . . ouch! Hard floor and bedsheets?

"Whoozit?" came sleepily from the dark.

"Mike?" My voice trembled.

"No, I'm Mike," he said, then snuffled twice and snored happily.

My heart started slowing. It had only been a dream. Joel wasn't trapped in a cave and I didn't have to rescue him. My head hurt where I had clunked out of bed trying to avoid the lion, the bedsheets had wrapped me like a mummy, and I was definitely not a Christian living in the catacombs below the ancient city of Rome. It almost served me right for reading old history to fall asleep.

Still groggy, I rolled over and pulled myself onto the bed, trying to decide what was bothering me so badly. A detail I was overlooking.

The moon's glow outlined everything in the room. Mike's bed and Ralphy's bed, the one I was using. I shook my head to clear it from the terror of my dream and remembered. Joel was indeed missing. Which explained the dream and my subconscious mind trying to solve the problem of where Carl was keeping him and Ralphy. If only finding Joel was as easy as having a maze of tunnels to look through.

Suddenly, that detail snapped into place. I laughed aloud.

"Mike! Mike! Wake up, pal!"

I sprang up and began shaking his shoulders.

"Not me. Honest, not me. A guy named Ricky did it."

"Wake up, chowderhead." I shook him again. Figures I was getting the blame for whatever trouble he was avoiding in his dream.

With a final groan, he left his sleep behind and slowly sat up.

"Take a deep breath," I instructed him.

He did. "Peee-eeewwwww."

"Exactly," I said. "Cats. Fifty-two of them."

I stood beside the open window. Our bedroom faced Doreen's house. The breeze that ruffled the curtains brought in the smell of her cats.

"Just think," Mike called across the room. "If you hadn't woken me, I never would have known. Now, I'm sure, the smell will help me stay awake all night."

"You'll thank me soon enough," I promised. "Especially if you use your brains. Why do we suddenly smell her cats? Because her windows are open too. Why all of a sudden now? The smell wasn't around earlier in the week."

I didn't explain to him my crazy dream about the lions. It was enough that the smell of cats had given the first clue to Joel's location.

Mike, in his Mickey Mouse decorated pajamas, joined me at the window to stare thoughtfully at Doreen's house.

"What you're saying is that someone else is in the house. Someone who needs fresh air and has opened Doreen's windows . . ."

". . . Someone who wants a convenient place to hide out and watch his own house. Someone with enough money at stake as a drug dealer to also become a kidnapper."

Mike whistled. "Would he kidnap Doreen too?"

I shrugged. "Why not. You can't get in more trouble for three people than two. And who would ever notice if Doreen was missing? She's got no family. Only cats."

"There's only one thing," Mike said. "We can watch the house forever, but we still need proof, any proof, to get the police to search her house."

He was right, of course.

I worried about it as I lay awake for most of the rest of the night. I worried about it all through church the next morning, when I should have been praying instead. And I worried about it all the way back from church, as Mike and Lisa and I walked in silence. Lisa for her reasons, and Mike and I for mine.

Then, as I was glumly changing from my Sunday suit into blue jeans and a T-shirt just before lunch, the proof tumbled down from the bedroom closet and hit me on the shoulders.

Joel's teddy bear. He never leaves home without it.

16

It took fifteen minutes to convince Dr. Manford to call the police. He wasn't as sure as I was about the significance of Joel's teddy bear. Mike and Lisa, however, knew what it meant to find it without Joel nearby, and their insistence finally changed Dr. Manford's mind.

Mike, Lisa, and I waited anxiously near the street for the police to arrive. That took another twenty minutes of early afternoon sunshine.

The entire time, I fought doubts in my mind. Again and again I told myself that our theory must be right. Doreen's house was the perfect place — except for the truckloads of cats — for Carl to hide kidnapped people and still watch the area.

Lisa and Mike kept staring at Doreen's house, as if looking hard enough would let them see through the walls. Lisa's face showed a brave and quiet sadness. I almost decided right then to tell her we knew how bad her dilemma was.

I should have.

My first inkling of disaster came with the startled looks on the faces of the two policeman who stepped out of the cruiser.

"You guys!" they said together.

Mike and I cringed.

The first cop then sighed and turned to his partner. "Sam, I been telling you this end of town is not for us. Something about the beach and the ocean that makes this job too goofy."

Naturally. The two cops who had rescued us from the three

hoods at THE BLUE PELICAN. Same grey crewcuts and heavy, middle-aged faces.

Their eyes returned to me. And stayed on me. Finally I realized why they were giving me such strange looks. I shifted Joel's teddy bear to my other hand and hid it behind my back.

"This is going to be good, Sam," the first one said.

"It sure is, Fred."

"It's not like you think," I said. "The kid who owns this teddy bear has been kidnapped—"

"Spare us, kid. The professor already gave us the details. If we'd have known it involved you guys . . ."

"Go easy, Sam. We're here. We might as well check it out."

Only the buzz of insects in the hot air broke the silence as all five of us walked to Doreen's front door.

She answered the knock almost instantly. The cat smell was faint behind her.

"Why hello, officers." She smiled sweetly. "And the lovely children from next door. I'm sorry I haven't had the chance to invite them over after our delightful conversation earlier this week."

Doreen wore a checked apron and her gray hair was pinned in the demure bun she had worn when we met her on the cliffs. Only I didn't remember the conversation as delightful.

Doreen continued cheerfully. "What can I do for all of you on this Sunday afternoon? Are you campaigning for charity?"

"No, ma'am," the officer named Sam said with respect as he removed his hat. He elbowed the other officer to do the same. "This is going to sound crazy, but we're here to investigate a kidnapping."

"Oh, my." Doreen's eyes widened. "That sounds frightening. I don't know how I can help you, but I would be happy to try."

The second cop, Fred, scuffed his shoes uncomfortably, like a little boy in front of a school teacher. "Well, actually ma'am, we heard that you were kidnapped, but obviously someone was playing a joke."

Sam glared down at Mike and I. It wasn't hard to figure out who they were going to blame for that.

I didn't care. My heart was heavy and dropping fast in new worry over Joel and Ralphy. If they weren't here, where could they be? Where would we look next? How long would Carl wait before deciding he couldn't wait any longer?

I barely heard the rest of the conversation. It wasn't until the door clicked shut that I realized the policemen were talking to me and Mike.

". . . we could have you both fined hundreds of dollars and—"

"Sam, let's just go. Remember your blood pressure. It's not worth getting worked up over a couple of brats."

With that, both of them strode away from us down the side-walk, their big leather shoes thumping out anger and disgust.

* * * * * * * *

When we returned, Dr. Manford raised an eyebrow as we trooped through the kitchen.

"I don't know whether to be relieved or not," he said. "I'm glad there wasn't a kidnapping, but I am rather embarrassed that the police had to be involved in this mistake. I hope you can have the patience to wait until tomorrow when Carl and the two boys get back from Hollywood."

I nodded. Nothing could convince me Joel and Ralphy weren't in danger, but disagreeing with Dr. Manford would get us nowhere.

"Well," he said, "I'd like to go for a walk. I'll see you all later." With that, Dr. Manford tightened his tie and walked outside.

Mike, Lisa, and I flopped into the family room. Lisa was still much quieter than usual.

I decided right then it was time to ask her about the patch-man, time to break the wall between us. Without Mike around. He's not famous for diplomacy.

"Mike," I said casually. "In yesterday's excitement, I forgot all about an article I photocopied at the library. It's about the Gentleman Pirate."

He brightened. I didn't give him a chance to speak. "In fact, it's in my room if you want to grab it." I thought hard, trying to recall where I had left it. "On my chair near the closet."

Mike gave me the look that said Get it yourself. I gave him the look that said Leave us here alone. He shrugged and shuffled out of the room and up the stairs.

Lisa continued staring at the dark blank television screen.

"Mike and I have kept something from you, Lisa. We know about the guy with the eye patch. The guy they call Big Joe."

She stiffened and turned her stare on me. "You know about Carl then."

"Yes. I also know your terrible dilemma."

"Ricky," she breathed with relief. As she slumped completely, I awkwardly walked over and put my hand on her shoulder. She pulled me beside her and wrapped her arms around me to quietly cry against my neck.

"I was so worried," she sobbed. "First Big Joe, then the note. And he made me promise not to say anything."

"We'll get through this somehow, no matter what it—"

"Hey guys!" Mike bounced into the room. "Cool letter."

His eyes left the paper he held and strayed to where I was trying to get my arms away from holding Lisa.

"Sick," Mike said. "If I want that kind of stuff, I'll watch soap operas."

Lisa giggled, the first sign of happiness I had seen in her since Big Joe had met her on the beach.

"One must comfort one's friends," I pointed out.

"Yeah, right. Anyway Ricky, you never told me about this cool letter. I thought you said it was a history article."

I frowned.

Mike walked over to Lisa and me, and held out the folded and worn piece of paper.

"This is a photocopy, but it's not the article," I said as I studied it.

"Genius. The boy's a genius."

"Where did you get this, Mike?"

"Not on your chair, pal. All it had was a wrinkled T-shirt."

"I've never seen this letter before, Mike. Where did you get it?"

He caught the intensity of my question and snapped out of his smirk. "I saw the edge of it sticking out from underneath a shirt you had thrown on the closet floor."

I read aloud the letter written in wavering ink. Age marks showed as dark streaks across the photocopy.

February 8, 1887

Dear Melissa,

It is during times like these that I am grateful to have a daughter such as you to cherish. I need your love more than ever. My soul is weary because of my sin, and without your understanding I shall be alone and cold in the world.

Your godfather, the Gentleman Pirate, has banished me from Pirate's Haven. Fairly so. When a friend of twenty years begins to pilfer from their shared treasure, the friend should be treated like vermin. My grief is so great, I almost wish the Gentleman Pirate would have ordered my execution.

You will not see me again. I am leaving here tonight by the Pirate's orders. Yet I must keep your love around me like a blanket. If you forgive me, a tired old man who has repented of his greed, I shall have that to comfort me as I wander.

As to the treasure, the Gentleman Pirate has promised that you will get my share. We have a map, and it is very plain to see for generations to come. It is a map in two pieces, and one piece is very close to you. When you wake in the morning, look for it, and think of me.

I dare not say more, should this letter fall into the wrong

hands. You of all people will know where to find that piece. And it is the same for the Gentleman Pirate.

Take care of yourself and may Our Lord in His infinite mercy watch over us both.

Joseph

My voice had dropped to a whisper as I finished reading. I was stunned. I didn't know where to start asking questions. So I explained what I knew.

"At the library yesterday, I found an article that told about the Gentleman Pirate and Joseph Dominga, the man who captained their ship. They accumulated a great treasure. Dominga, in the end, started stealing from it and was caught and banished. Dominga was murdered shortly after, the Gentleman Pirate died of pneumonia six months later, and no treasure map or treasure was found."

Mike whistled. "Then this is Dominga's final letter!"

"Yes," I said. "Historians believe there was no treasure map at all. That the treasure was lost forever. This letter proves different!"

Lisa brought us back to earth. "Yes, sir. If the letter is authentic, we'll have millions. There's only the detail of finding a treasure map that's been hidden for a hundred years."

Silence. With reality back, the other questions in my mind returned.

"I can't understand what this letter was doing in my closet. Or where my article went." I snapped my fingers and answered myself.

"Of course. The closet. That's where I found Joel's teddy bear."

"Huh?" Lisa and Mike said at the same time.

I leaned forward. "Here's the theory. Carl's looking for the treasure. Either Ralphy and Joel stumble onto something about his drug operation, or across this letter, or both. So Carl has to kidnap them. Ralphy's smart enough to leave behind the teddy bear and letter as a clue and ..."

I stopped. Lisa's ice cold stare felt like a truck pushing me into a brick wall.

"What'd I say wrong?"

She stood. "How dare you accuse my Uncle Carl of dealing drugs. Or of kidnapping Ralphy and Joel. You've made dumb jokes before, but this one is enough to make me wonder about what kind of friend you really are."

"B-b-but Big Joe! You said he told you everything. I thought you knew and—"

"No," she corrected me with blazing eyes. "You said you knew everything. And then tricked me into thinking you wanted to help my poor Uncle Carl."

"What is going on," Mike demanded. "Somebody please start talking English."

Lisa and I stared at each other. Finally she said, "Let's start over. At the beginning. Big Joe will understand if I break my promise."

17

I nodded, and explained to her all we knew about Carl, including the money, the midnight meeting that now seemed so long ago, how we had been afraid Big Joe had kidnapped her the day before, and our fear that Carl had been blackmailing her into silence.

Lisa bit her lip doubtfully. "Suddenly, I'm not sure who to believe. You see, all Big Joe told me was that Carl was in trouble. Big enough trouble that he needed me to call him day or night if I heard anything from Carl."

"If?" Mike asked. "Not when?"

"That's what made me so afraid. Big Joe said the police couldn't be called yet. And he said I had to keep it a secret."

I didn't want to say it, but I had to. "Lisa, doesn't it sound like they have something to hide? Something . . . criminal?"

She bit her lip again. "That's why I'm not sure who to believe."

"Did you tell Big Joe about the note from Carl?"

"Yes," Lisa said. "I called him last night. He said thanks and he would find a way to let me know what was happening later."

I wanted to punch a wall. So much confusion. How could a person make sense of it? I spoke my thoughts aloud.

"We have three possibilities. One, Carl is not a drug dealer, and he and Ralphy and Joel are in some kind of trouble we can't understand until Big Joe tells us more. Two, Carl is a drug dealer, and he really has taken Ralphy and Joel, just like Mike and I really thought. Or three, Carl actually did take Ralphy and

Joel to Hollywood and they'll be back tomorrow."

Mike protested. "But if he did take them to Hollywood, Big Joe wouldn't have approached Lisa."

I nodded. "So we're down to two possibilities. For Lisa's sake, I hope Carl isn't a drug dealer. Which would mean, though, we have no idea where to look for the three of them."

Lisa closed her eyes and spoke in a low, pained voice. "Uncle Carl did kidnap Ralphy and Joel. And he does have them next door at Doreen's, like you thought all along."

How could she suddenly be so certain?

"Don't you think Doreen's behavior was strange when the police knocked at the door?" she continued. "She was so sweet, so nice. So unlike the Doreen we first met halfway down the cliff."

"Mike, kick me hard," I said. "Because I can't kick myself."

Mike shook his head. "Not unless you kick me back. I missed it too, Ricky. Doreen said our first conversation had been delightful, that she was sorry she hadn't had a chance to invite us over. And remember, she answered the door almost instantly. Almost as if . . ."

"As if someone was behind her, with a threat to hurt Ralphy and Joel if she didn't get the police to leave." How could I have missed it?

Lisa's voice still reflected pain. "Exactly. So she did the next best thing. She lied about our meeting, hoping we would see that something was wrong."

I groaned loudly as another thought hit. "Mike, please, please kick me. There's one thing so obvious, I should have checked it yesterday."

"What's that?"

"Carl's Jeep. If it's not around, we haven't proven a thing. But if we find it nearby, then we know for sure he's next door."

Later, I would wonder how things might have been different if we would have looked for the Jeep immediately upon reading

Carl's note. As it was, we found it five minutes later, parked in Doreen's dim and dusty garage, draped under a few old blankets.

The rest of the Sunday went very slowly. Lisa remained quiet from seeing her uncle in a new way — as a drug dealer desperate enough to kidnap her friends. Mike's jaw stayed clenched for hours; he preferred direct action to waiting. And I worried and wondered how long we could wait before Carl got tired of holding Ralphy and Joel. It wasn't until I had been lying awake in bed that night for nearly an hour that I thought of a way to get the police into Doreen's house without a search warrant. Then, despite my worry for Ralphy and Joel, I fell asleep smiling.

* * * * * * * *

"Don't ask questions, Mike." I reviewed my memory of Doreen's stone shed. The Monday morning had turned out, as usual, bright and cheerful. Which I definitely did not feel. "The burlap potato bags are in a pile in the corner of the shed. Grab as many as you can carry, and meet us down at the beach."

"I wish you'd give us a hint," he grumbled. "I thought we were rescuing Ralphy and Joel."

"Patience, pal." I wished I was as confident as I sounded. Carl's deep sea fishing rod was on the ground beside us.

I turned to Lisa. "You've got the string, both steaks, and a knife?"

She lifted a clear plastic bag for my inspection, showing everything in place. "I still think you should call the police again. Or tell Dr. Manford. I mean, with the Jeep there, we have more proof."

I shook my head. "Doreen could easily say she lent her car to Carl for the weekend. Dr. Manford would find a reason too. Nobody's exactly in a trusting mood after yesterday."

We had just finished breakfast. Dr. Manford had left immediately after, for some research at the University of San Diego archives. We stood in the morning sun in Carl's backyard. The grass was still wet with dew.

I carried the fishing rod in my left hand and a knot of worry in my stomach. If the first part of my plan didn't work out . . .

"Let's go," I urged, blocking out the thought. "Mike, meet us at the flat rock where we had our picnic lunch."

He grumbled as he walked away, but met Lisa and me only a few minutes after we had arrived at the edge of the beach.

Sea gulls wheeled over our heads, screaming out their usual curiosity and hunger.

In front of us was the flat rock. I stepped backwards until we were hidden behind another boulder roughly fifty feet away. Mike and Lisa followed slowly. I was reluctant to tell them what I had in mind because I was afraid they would laugh and walk away.

For a moment, I almost called it off. Plans often seem great at night, when you are only thinking about them, and you don't have to test them in the cold reality of daytime. Worse, this plan relied on two long shots, and we were about to try the first.

I took a deep breath.

"Mike, will you cut a mouse-sized piece of steak?"

He sadly shook his head at my obvious loss of sanity, but took the plastic bag from Lisa.

"Lisa, you need to have about two feet of string ready. Hold it between your teeth. You'll need both hands for the potato sack."

Mike handed me the chunk of steak. I carefully tied fishing line around the middle of it.

I grinned a grin I didn't feel inside. "Watch this!" I said, then hoped it would work.

With both hands on the fishing rod, I flung the meat through the air. The reel whirred lightly as the line stripped from it. It wasn't heavy enough to carry far, but there was a breeze at our back, and it helped drift the small chunk of steak just enough to land on the edge of the rock.

Even I wasn't ready for what happened next.

Within an instant, a huge gull swept down and scooped the

meat as it was skidding to a stop. That gull was almost too late. Three other gulls were at its tail feathers, screaming rage at having missed the food. The first gull, barely pausing on the rock, flung its head back without hesitation and gulped the meat in a single gobble. Then it streaked into the air, with the same flurry of gulls in hot pursuit.

I gave it another two seconds of flying time, enough so that the chunk of meat was deep inside. Then I set the drag on the reel and pulled gently.

"Scraaaaaawwwwwww! Scraaaaawwwwww!" The gull almost cartwheeled in mid-air at the unexpected yank of fishing line. It recovered just before hitting the sand, and by that time I had frantically reeled in five yards of fishing line.

"Scraaaaaawwwwwww! Scraaaaawwwwww!" Its widespread wings buffeted the air. I was glad for the heavy-duty line on Carl's deep sea rod. The rod strained hard against my hands.

"Scraaaaaawwwwwww! Scraaaaawwwwww!" So far my guess had been right. The gull was too greedy and the line was too tight and it was fighting too hard for it to even consider spewing the meat back out again.

The fight was intense, but beyond it I became conscious of another sensation. Mike pounding my back with glee. He hollered in joy.

"Bring him in, pal! Bring in him, bronco buster!"

He was right. The gull bucked and fought the air like a wild stallion.

Two minutes, three minutes, finally four minutes later, I had reeled the gull in close enough for us to see its cold yellow eyes blinking in rage. Ten feet away and suspended by terrible flapping barely head height off the ground, it pulled in a tug-of-war that I didn't dare draw tighter.

"The sack, Lisa," I panted. "Move behind and throw the sack over it!"

She scrambled for position on the sand. The gull tried veering away, but could not. The line was too tight, the rod arched too hard.

Lisa avoided the scrabbling wings and brought the gull down to earth with a fling of the burlap. As soon as the bag closed darkness upon it, the gull stopped struggling. And finally, it regurgitated the piece of steak.

By pulling the fishing line, I drew the steak gently from a tiny opening at the top of the sack before Lisa tightened the string completely.

"Our bait's none the worse for wear," I said as casually as I could. "Time for the next one."

"Come on, pal. Let me give this one a try."

"I'm not sure, Mike. This was my idea. And you weren't keen about helping out."

What he didn't know was that I was tired enough to beg him to take over. Gulls put up a better fight than bass.

"Just once. I'll even pay . . ."

The magic words.

"I still don't know, Mike."

"I'll cut your lawn for an entire month when we get back to Jamesville."

I reeled in my line completely, and drew the rod back as if I were prepared to cast. My arms were bricks, and it took effort not to show my fatigue.

"I'll even rake."

I set the rod down. "And weed the garden?"

He nodded.

"Sure, Mike," I said with a generous grin. "And Lisa can do the next sea gull. We'll take turns."

By the time Mike reeled in his first sea gull, he knew by the weight of his tired arms that he'd been taken. But, as I reminded him many times later on from my Jamesville hammock as I watched him hoe the garden, a deal's a deal.

18

Climbing an aluminum ladder and carrying three sacks of sea gulls is not the easiest thing in the world. Not when any one of a dozen gulls inside the burlap becomes irate at the darkness and bouncing around, and savagely and randomly pecks at your rear end which happens to be on the other side.

"Yeeoww!" I hissed to myself.

After three hard hours of sea gull fishing, though, I was almost at the point of not caring whether or not someone heard me. Filling nine potato sacks full takes careful work. You have to fight the sea gull to a midair standstill, then sneak up behind it and grab. If you miss and fail to trap its wings against its body, you add more scratches to your face and have a much tougher time sneaking up again. Once you have the gull, then you have to be quick about getting it into the bag before the other trapped ones fly out. The only good thing about it is their greed and hunger — it doesn't take long to interest a new gull in steak.

Fortunately for us, seagulls look much bigger than they weigh. Their bones are light and most of their bulk is in their wings. We had each carried 60 or 70 pounds of sea gulls back up the cliffs. We had split the load into three sacks each, tied together at the top and slung over our shoulders. Which had meant a lot of disgruntled pecking along the way. I felt like a dart board.

Now we were on the verge of seeing exactly how long the second long shot might be. I had told Mike and Lisa the plan only after they promised not to laugh or quit halfway through.

The ladder trembled with every step I took, and I was only halfway up. As I climbed, an idle part of me sourly noted the good weather. Who cared about Southern California dream days when a kid brother and a best friend were in danger? The sky was a crisp pale blue, and a light breeze, as usual, came in from the ocean, to take away enough of the heat of the sun to make it perfect. With the green-gray haze of faraway hills, Southern California was as pretty as I always dreamed. If only I could have a guarantee that Ralphy and Joel were still fine.

"Yeeouch!" I grunted at another sudden peck to my hind end. *You'll have a chance to peck soon enough, pal,* I mentally told the disrespectful sea gull through gritted teeth; *save your energy for then.*

Its moment arrived two rungs higher.

I left two bags slung front and back over my shoulders, one tied to the other. The third bag I held tight in my right hand. That freed my left hand to work the third-story hallway window.

I reached in and fumbled with the latch and slowly pushed open the window.

"Phewwww." I nearly jumped away at the strong closeup dose of cat smell.

Then I waited. My watch read five minutes past the hour. I had arrived with two minutes to spare.

Two cats in the hallway sauntered past the window. They were so big and fat and secure that they didn't even bother glancing my way. I waited longer. Three other cats wandered by.

I thought of Lisa and how I had been overwhelmed earlier by affection for her and her quiet braveness. She knew very well that a successful rescue mission would also condemn her uncle as a drug dealer and kidnapper. Yet she was as determined as Mike and I, and as I now waited, she was waiting too, poised by a basement window with her own three sacks of gulls.

Just when I thought I couldn't wait longer, it came. Mike's fake owl hoot.

I hoisted the sack to the window, and lowered it to the floor. I did the same as quickly as possible without dropping them with the other two sacks.

Then with one hard tug each, I jerked the string away from the tops of the sacks.

I slammed the window shut, and did a hop slide down each step of the ladder. My feet slammed the ground, but I was far from safe. I eased the ladder down to the grass and scrambling, I pulled on the ropes that worked the ladder extension, retracting the sliding parts so that it became compact again. Without pausing, I struggled to lift and balance the ladder well enough so that I could do a shambling run across Doreen's yard and back to Carl's garage.

Lisa and Mike were waiting. They pulled open the door so I didn't have to stop.

I gasped for breath. "Successful?"

They both nodded.

"Lisa made the calls?" I panted out another question.

Lisa nodded.

"No problems at the kitchen window, Mike?"

He shook his head.

"Then let me get my breath back. That ladder was heavy."

I leaned forward and placed my hands on my hips and drew as much air as possible into my lungs. Part of my heavy panting, I knew, came from fear. What if the plan didn't work?

Lisa simply gazed calmly at me. Mike paced the garage, going from the dusty window where he stared at Doreen's house, and back to me where he scowled with impatience.

Finally, I could breathe normally. I gave them my most confident smile. "Time to look innocent."

"About time," Mike said. "This wait is killing me."

19

We arrived at the front lawn of Doreen's house all at the same time. Police. Firemen. Dogcatchers. SPCA authorities. Newspaper photographers. Mike. Lisa. Me. Sea gulls. And cats. A leaping army of cats.

The police cruised up with lights flashing, no sirens. The firemen screamed into sight with fire-engine lights flashing and sirens howling. The dogcatchers approached cautiously—no lights, no sirens— but on seeing the front lawn alive with cats, they immediately opened doors and readied long poles with nets. The SPCA people slowly parked their plain grey sedan, stepped out, and blinked in confusion. The newspaper photographer had his camera clicking even as he sprinted to get the best view.

Mike, Lisa, and I tried to look as if all this was a surprise.

The fire-engine siren wound down slowly, even as neighbors poured out from their houses in all directions. And as the sirens slowly lost volume, we finally heard.

It was an illusion, I knew, but the house seemed to pop and crackle from the full-scale warfare taking place inside. The degree of that warfare we could only guess at by the way its soldiers escaped like popcorn from a hot pan.

"Wow," Mike said. "The track meet is on!"

Cats yowled, screeched, hissed, and scrambled in all directions. They poured from window ledges and from the suddenly slammed-open front door. They leaped to balconies and rain gutters. They leaped from balconies and rain gutters.

On their tails were sea gulls. Angry, spitting, screaming sea gulls. Pouring from the same windows and streaming from the same open front door. Following the wave of sea gulls came the next round of cats, snapping and pawing at tail feathers with insane fury.

They were animals fleeing a burning forest with no regard for obstacles in front. Not even for the newspaper photographer who made the mistake of getting too close to the front door and kneeling for a close-up shot.

They swarmed him like rats from a ship, beating a path over him as if he didn't exist. A sea gull mistook the thatch of his brown-gray hair for the fur of a cat, and it stopped long enough to haul out a beakfull. The photographer's outraged yell was lost in the yowling and screeching that boiled around him.

He struggled into a sitting position and Hezekiah, moving too fast to stop, pounded him back into the grass. More cats streamed over and around him.

"Oops," Mike said thoughtfully for the photographer.

Cats filled the lawn. Some stopped in a daze, unsure of what to do with their freedom after years of being cooped in Doreen's house. Others only picked up speed and became blurs of fur shooting between bushes, parked vehicles, and the legs of a fast-growing crowd. Shouts and squeals and jumps from people on the sidewalk only made for more noise and confusion.

The sea gulls? Most buzzed for open sky upon tumbling out of the house. A few of the really irritated ones turned back to divebomb the dazed cats who were too dumb to leave the lawn.

Added to all of that, police whistles blew. Dogcatchers tripped and fell over each other and fought bulging full nets of cats. The cats in the nets fought each other. An elderly SPCA woman lifted the bottom of her pants and walked onto the lawn and swatted a fireman for slapping a cat which had tried climbing his leg. Then she screamed and kicked at two other cats which tried using *her* for a tree.

And still more cats and sea gulls fled the house.

"You know," I said to no one in particular, "if Ralphy and Joel aren't in there, we're in bigger trouble than I can imagine."

My apparent calmness was the result of fright that verged on hysteria and left me powerless to move.

"Thanks, pal," Mike said. "You pick great times to second-guess your plans."

"Ninety sea gulls and fifty-two cats," Lisa said in awe. "I never dreamed it would be like this."

"Neither did I." My voice came from far away, like it belonged to someone else.

The last attack wave had boiled out of the house. The hush became an eerie quiet as everybody—police, firemen, SPCA authorities, spectators, cats, and sea gulls—reacted to the shock of what had just occurred.

Then the groan of the photographer broke the silence. A few cats yowled halfheartedly from the dogcatchers' nets, but mainly to check if they were still alive. The crowd started moving again, and people spoke in discreet whispers, pointing and waving their hands.

Two policemen strode to me and Mike and Lisa.

Absolute and total fear locked my knees as their faces sagged in recognition. Sam and Fred, jaws tight with anger.

"My question, kid, is not if you were behind this," Sam said as he placed his ham of a hand on my shoulder and squeezed slowly. "It's how. Then why."

"Me, sir? I heard all the noise and thought I'd come out here and take a look." That, I told myself, wasn't a lie.

Mike tried his hundred-watt grin. "Quite something, wasn't it, sir? Who'd have thought there could be so many cats in one house? And a sea gull invasion. What a freak of nature. I mean you have to wonder why a flock would suddenly decide to go cat hunting and all."

Fred put his hand on Mike's shoulder. "What a coincidence,

hey kid? You'd also have to wonder how all of us who arrived here managed to get anonymous phone calls begging for help."

"That is a bit strange, isn't it, sir."

Suddenly, the cop in front of me leaned in to place his face within two inches of mine. "Kid, I want the truth. And I want it now. If you mess around for another two seconds, I'll make sure you're in a delinquency school until you're gray and wrinkled."

I didn't let him wait to the two-second mark. An anger inside me from the fear for Joel's safety kept me from squirming. I said as directly as I could, "I think my brother is in serious danger, and after yesterday, this was the only way we could get anybody to look inside the house."

The cop stood and slapped his leg in frustration. "A stupid martyr! How you kids get those ideas in your head is beyond me. No matter how right you believed you were, you're still going to pay, and pay very—"

"Sir?" Lisa politely pulled at the cop's sleeve. "Sir? Would you mind turning around?"

What I saw and what I had missed during the heat of the cop's anger was something that nearly made me cry as I looked in the direction of Lisa's pointing arm.

Ralphy and Joel leaned on each other as they slowly moved down the front steps of Doreen's house. Behind them, pale and very uncertain, shuffled Carl and Doreen.

I couldn't help myself. I shook myself loose from the cop's grip and sprinted forward.

"Joel!" I shouted. "Ralphy!"

When I got there, I could say nothing else. I just held their hands and grinned.

Carl coughed from behind them. I had forgotten about him.

"Thanks for rescuing us," he croaked. "Without you, I'm not sure we would have left there alive."

20

"Sleep much?" Mike grinned as he flopped across the bed in the master bedroom.

Ralphy snorted. "With all those dogs barking during an all-night cat smorgasbord? Not a chance."

I ignored them. It was Tuesday morning. After all the excitement of the rescue the day before, the dullness of getting back to work seemed even duller.

"Come on, guys," Lisa said. "I'll bet it's not funny to Doreen. She loves her cats."

"Don't worry, Lisa," I said quietly. "The dogs were doing her a favor. I'm sure all of the cats headed straight home as soon as they were chased."

That satisfied her, so I resumed my morose contemplation of the work ahead of us, the work we had already delayed once. Sanding a ceiling. Yuck. And those stupid grooves looked at least a quarter inch deep. Sanding is the lousiest job a person can find. Your arms ache within seconds, and all the dust drops into your eyes and mouth, but there's no way to stop breathing as you sand, so you either get throatfuls or nostrilfuls of the stuff.

"I can't work," Mike declared from his comfortable position on the bed.

"So tell me something new."

"I'm serious," he insisted to me. "We simply don't have enough answers around here and it's driving me crazy."

Lisa smiled. "But the most important question was answered.

I'm so grateful that Carl isn't a drug dealer."

My face started turning red, the way it had been for three hours straight yesterday afternoon after we realized Carl too had been a kidnap victim.

It had taken a half hour of excited discussion to find out exactly what had happened.

On Saturday, while I was in the library, and while Mike and Lisa were at the beach, Ralphy had left Joel in the house briefly to explore the site near the pirate's tunnel. Without warning, on his way there, he had stumbled across two huge men tying Doreen's arms together as they began to kidnap her. Before Ralphy could react, the men had grabbed him, and tied his arms together too. To make it worse, as the men were leading Ralphy and Doreen back up the cliff, Carl accidentally appeared. Carl made it as far as his yard before they tackled him and dragged him back.

After they had Doreen, Ralphy, and Carl safely captured in Doreen's house, they left again to find Joel. The men knew that with Joel kidnapped too, they could type the note—on Carl's typewriter—that made it look like Carl and the boys were in Hollywood.

Joel, who is quiet but definitely not stupid, knew immediately that the two strangers entering the house in a sneaky way were bad news. Or maybe he had seen them tackle Carl earlier. Either way, he knew he should hide.

Once again I realized how important his teddy bear is to him. Sensing danger, he had bravely decided to hide the teddy bear first. Joel had moved the chair to the closet and placed the bear on the top shelf. Then he hid himself in the closet. The poor kid never realized that leaving the chair in front was a dead giveaway.

The kidnappers had locked Ralphy and Joel in one room, and Doreen and Carl in another just down the hall. They had tied them all to chairs and taken turns guarding the hallway.

Wrong about Carl, at least I had been right about the smell. The kidnappers could not get rid of the cats. That would have drawn too much attention to the house. They had opened the windows a few inches instead. Enough to get air into the house. Not enough so the cats could escape.

When the ruckus between sea gulls and cats started, and the sirens had approached, both men had opted for quick getaways out the back door. In the confusion, they were certain not to be noticed. And, of course, they hadn't been.

Carl had taken that opportunity to knock his door down to the hallway. Only an hour earlier, he had finished fraying his rope clean through against an edge of the windowsill in the bedroom, quickly untied Doreen, and they had decided to wait because he knew of the posted guard. With them gone, it was easy for him to kick open the doors, untie Ralphy and Joel, and help them out of the house. Or easier than jumping out, anyway, even with the cats and sea gulls fighting World War III around them.

That's when Carl had thanked us at the front door for the rescue. And also when I had blurted out, "Arrest that man! He is wrecking the nation by selling drugs!"

Ralphy had shaken his head *no! no! no!* but it had been too late. My words had come out, and I had lamely tried to explain the drug dealer theory, even as Ralphy kept shaking his head.

Cop one and cop two at that point had rolled their eyeballs in disgust and shooed Mike and me away, choosing instead to gently help Doreen away from the disaster that was the inside of her house, and over to Carl's where food and liquid and soft chairs were the most important priority after their ordeal.

Thinking over that, I spoke slowly. "Mike, we've got two days left until our trip is finished. Yes, I'd like to get a lot of questions answered. But we also have to pay our way."

I pointed at the ceiling and the dumb grooves which needed sanding.

Mike gave a last try at delaying our start. "But what about the pirate's treasure? What about Carl's real reason for the bag of money? What about Doreen's determination not to tell us why she had been kidnapped?"

"Don't worry, Mike. I spent half of last night trying to figure things out." I had tried to sort through odds and ends of little clues which tugged at the edges of my mind but stayed stubbornly elusive. There was a pattern somewhere, but I couldn't put the one piece into place that would—

"And?" Mike never gives a guy time to think.

"Besides the coins and letter and Big Joe, there's Doreen. Who kidnapped her? Why, for crying out loud. Worse, it's suddenly occurred to me that her living in that big old house is very strange to begin with."

"Because of the cats?" Lisa asked.

I shook my head. "Because of money. Big houses overlooking the ocean cost a pile of money. Doreen doesn't work. She merely wanders around the cliffs and . . . "

A stray thought hit me, but I shook it off. Not possible, I told myself. On the other hand, maybe it was.

" . . . and EEEEEEP!"

The single tug on my blue jean belt loop, coming so unexpectedly while I was deep in thought, nearly had me jumping into a paint bucket.

"Joel," I began sternly.

He smiled, teddy bear tucked under one arm.

"Funny lines," he said pointing at the ceiling.

"Brilliant, Sherlock," I told him.

"Funny lines in the cat house too," he continued gravely. Then stared upward with a puzzled look on his face, the same look he has when grown-ups do something strange.

"Then good thing Doreen doesn't want her house painted," Mike growled. "One job like this is enough."

Ralphy stood hesitantly, his own face a perplexed squint. "Joel's right. They locked us in a bedroom that had the same kind of grooved lines on the ceiling. I guess I didn't think about it because I was so scared."

Slowly, so slowly it was like the sun rising, a certainty dawned across me. Then, as I realized what it meant, my legs grew weak. Almost as if dreaming, I lurched to the window ledge and leaned against it to stare out at the ocean.

Did I dare say it out loud? Yes, but slowly and in a voice I didn't trust not to tremble.

"Mike, you can rest easy about ever having to sand the ceiling," I said without looking back at them.

"Great. Why?"

"One mystery is solved."

"Naturally. Just like that."

I turned and grinned. "Lisa, what's the first thing you see in the morning when you wake?"

"The ceiling."

"Right. Listen."

I pulled the letter from my pocket, the one he had found on the floor of the closet. I read from the middle of it.

"'As to the treasure, the Gentleman Pirate has promised that you will get my share. We have a map, and it is very plain to see for generations to come. It is a map in two pieces, and one piece is very close to you. When you wake in the morning, look for it, and think of me.'"

Mike grinned back at me.

"That's right, pal," I said. "A two-piece map. In plain sight. On bedroom ceilings in neighboring houses."

21

"Don't ask me to explain yet. Just don't tell anybody what we're doing until I get back."

They looked at me as if I were crazy. I laughed as I moved away from the window and back to the center of the bedroom.

"Lisa, you're good at drawing. You and Ralphy get into Doreen's house. It shouldn't be hard. The cleaning crew is over there right now. Sketch out the lines on her ceiling. Come back here, and sketch out these lines. Mike and I will meet you in two hours."

"We will? I mean, we will."

"Yup." I paused. "And Ralphy, will you take Joel with you? Keep a firm grip on his teddy bear. The last thing we need right now is him to disappear."

They continued to look at me as if I were crazy.

I was so certain of all the things that had tumbled into place, I didn't mind for a second.

* * * * * * * *

"Doreen," I said, casually dropping the folded piece of paper onto the kitchen table, "here's the letter those kidnappers stole from you."

"What sort of nonsense are you talking about?" She had stayed the night in a spare bedroom at Carl's house. The rescue, and the rest, had not made her any sweeter toward us. After all—as she pointed out every five minutes—it had been our sea gulls attacking her cats.

Dr. Manford yawned. "I hope this doesn't become another tedious game. Really. I'm a fair man, but I have important research and you kids . . ."

". . . were the ones to rescue us." Carl spoke gently but firmly. "If they want to call a conference to announce the moon is made of cheese, they're welcome to it."

I didn't blame Dr. Manford for being irritated. After all, there was still enough cat dander on Doreen's clothes to make him sneeze occasionally. And after every fifth or sixth honking blow of his nose, he pulled out a new, crisply folded handkerchief and threw the old one away.

Dr. Manford smiled. "Of course, Carl. I'm sorry."

Carl sat opposite us. In between were Ralphy and Lisa on one side. Mike and Joel and his teddy bear on the opposite.

All eyes were upon me. *What was it about those handkerchiefs?*

"Please get on with it," Dr. Manford said, smile in place.

"Yes, sir. It's about Doreen's letter."

"Rubbish," she snapped. She pushed a wisp of gray hair back from her face.

"I hope not, ma'am. Because I believe it was your grandmother's letter."

Ralphy and Lisa shot startled glances at each other. It's nice to be able to surprise your friends.

Doreen's eyes narrowed, so I pressed on. "In fact, if it wasn't for your letter, we would never have found the Gentleman Pirate's treasure map."

Put that in your pipe and smoke it, I thought as Doreen and Dr. Manford leaned forward in sudden excitement.

"Hah, hah," Dr. Manford laughed weakly and sat back again. "What kids will do for entertainment."

Doreen reached across the table and took the letter in her gnarled and trembling hands. "You really have found the treasure map, haven't you. I can hear it in your voice."

I nodded.

"I've devoted most of my adult life to its search. Alone and too greedy to dare let anyone help." Her harsh and defiant face softened in sadness as she continued. "I've almost become a hermit, not daring to share my knowledge or my letter. The treasure is so immense, I thought it would be worth the price. What's strange is now that you have a map, I know I was wrong. Look at me. No love. No husband. No children. And always suspicious."

I pretended not to see the tear that left a shiny path down her sun-worn skin.

"Joseph Dominga is your great-grandfather," I stated.

She chuckled, despite the single tear that had become a stream. "Great-great grandfather. Surely I'm not so old to merely be a great-granddaughter."

"This is fascinating," Dr. Manford murmured. "It can help my research so much."

"Don't leave us hanging, Ricky," Carl said. "How'd you guess all this?"

"Buried sacks of cat litter."

Carl chortled as Doreen blushed.

"Actually sir, it was all the questions. Where did Joel find pirates' coins? How did the letter get on my closet floor? Who owned it? One way or another, all of them pointed to the treasure. When I wondered why Doreen was kidnapped, I wondered if that too involved the treasure. Then I remembered where we first met Doreen. On the cliffs."

"Scoundrels," Doreen stated with a crooked grin.

"Yes. We caught you digging. But you had an excuse. Burying cat litter. And as soon as I wondered if you were really looking for treasure instead, everything else made sense. Including the pirate coins."

Doreen's face brightened. "They're not lost?"

"You carried them in your pockets all the time, didn't you?"

She folded the letter abruptly and stared hard. "How did you know? Unless you—"

"Stole them? No ma'am. Before we saw you that first time on the cliffs, we heard you." I replayed the sounds in my head. A scuffle, then a sharp *clink-clink* before the shovel hit the ground. "Looking back, once I guessed who you might be, the clinking in your pocket made more sense, especially in trying to decide where Joel found the coins without finding a treasure. You must have lost them some time later that afternoon. Joel being Joel found them on one of his countless scouting trips."

"I tripped in my backyard while chasing Hezekiah," Doreen said. "For some reason, he was all worked up when I returned that afternoon. They must have fallen out then." She peered at my face, then Mike's. She grinned. "Those scratches! One of you two scoundrels had gotten his dander up."

"Yes. Later, we found a tun—" I stopped myself as something tiny and solid thunked my arm. A ladybug. It shook itself twice to collect its balance, then began wandering downward. I walked to the open window and brushed it away into the backyard. "Yes," I started over. "We found a—"

I stopped again, this time puzzled at something racing through my mind.

Ladybug. Ladybug. What should the ladybug have been telling me? Suddenly, I needed to be alone. Something about the ladybug nagged at me, and I wanted to sort it out.

"Hang on," Carl said, snapping me out of my thoughts. "Let me see if I can go from there. If Doreen was indeed looking for treasure, it would follow that she was the owner of the letter. And that the letter—and treasure—was a good enough reason for her to be kidnapped. Which would also explain why she was reluctant to talk about their reasons for doing it."

Doreen nodded.

"Plus the only other people to be near the closet were Joel's kidnappers. They must have dropped it there."

"Yes, sir."

"But how could you be sure Doreen was related to Joseph Dominga?"

"We weren't. But this morning, Mike and I went to the court-house and asked them to search land titles. Because I wondered if Doreen had inherited the house. Sure enough. The first regis-tered owner was Melissa Dominga, the girl in the letter. The house had not been sold since, was merely passed down through wills."

"Three generations of us have been searching . . ." Doreen's voice trailed away as she lost herself in thought.

Dr. Manford spoke again. "You guys are whiz kids, all right. But how can you be so sure about the map? And where, pray tell, is it?"

"The letter said the map was in two pieces, and to look for it when you wake up. The room Ralphy and Joel were in had the same weird lines on the ceiling as in Carl's bedroom. Lisa has sketched the patterns of both sets of lines and put them together."

Lisa grinned as she placed her drawings on the kitchen table. "The sketching was simple to do. There isn't much there. But you can see how both ceiling patterns can be arranged to make an entire map."

She folded one piece of paper and lined it up against the other. It formed a very simple map. At the top right was a round circle. In the middle was a tall rocket-like shape. The bottom left of the map held an X. Another line ran from the X, touched the tip of the rocket, and continued to the round circle.

The excitement that had filled the air in the kitchen suddenly faded as Dr. Manford spoke. "Nice theory. But it's obvious to anyone that those few lines aren't a map. Why, there's so little information that X could be anywhere in a hundred miles of coastline."

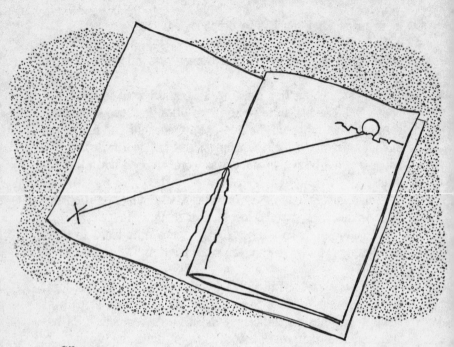

Silence.

Doreen slumped back in her chair. Carl scratched his goatee thoughtfully. Joel glanced outside hopefully, wanting his freedom. Mike and Lisa and Ralphy and I could only stare at the table.

Then Ralphy giggled.

We gave him a dirty look.

He giggled louder.

"For pity sake," Dr. Manford said.

Ralphy just kept giggling.

"He's got it figured," I said. "Ralphy's got it figured!"

Ralphy nodded.

"Out with it, man," Mike demanded.

Ralphy's eyes shone. "The legend also says the treasure will be found, quote, 'In the sight of all who care to open their eyes at the break of summer dawn,' unquote."

"We know that," Dr. Manford said. "That's where you found the map. Opening your eyes at dawn is waking up."

Ralphy shook his head and giggled again.

Then it hit me. I knew that rocket shape. I giggled with Ralphy.

"Enough! Enough!" Carl protested. "Out with it."

"It's a double clue, sir. Right, Ralphy?"

Ralphy nodded.

I closed my eyes to speak. "At the break of dawn tomorrow, the sun, rising in the east, will peek over the edge of those cliffs."

I looked at the map again, with the tiny circle and a line drawn from it across the top of the rocket, down to the X. "When the sun hits the huge outcrop of a rock shaped like a tall needle, it will cast a shadow and ..."

I let Ralphy finish.

He said proudly, "... And where that shadow touches down, it will mark a big fat X."

22

"Can you believe Mike being too sick to join us?" Ralphy asked as we picked our way down the cliffs. "This is the event of a lifetime, and he has to miss it. Poor guy."

I nodded and concentrated on my footing. The gray light just before sunrise gave few shadows to highlight the uneven ground, and walking with a heavy shovel in one hand was tricky.

Ahead of us, Dr. Manford led the way. He was followed by Lisa, who held Joel's hand. Behind Ralphy and me were Carl and Doreen. They whispered together as they walked.

My heart pounded as we approached the huge rock. Then we were there. We all stared upward at the edge of the cliff. The sun would break through any moment, and then it would take a quick and careful search to find where the shadow touched. If we missed the location, even by several yards, we might dig fruitlessly for days.

Then the sun's first ray appeared! Summer dawn had broken!

"Yeeeehah!" Ralphy shouted as he chased to find the shadow. He was still proud of having figured out the clue to the map. "It's here!" he shouted. "It's here."

"Where do they get the energy," I heard Doreen grumble to Carl. He patted her hand and smiled.

Strange, I thought to myself, *Doreen looks about ten years younger. Must be the thought of finding the treasure.*

I climbed and reached Dr. Manford, who was surveying a small plateau carefully.

"Hmmm. This does look like a logical spot. Why don't we try the exact center."

I dug one shovelful and as I was throwing the dirt to the side, something caught my eye.

"Should we try here first, sir?" I pointed to a small rock, about knee high, half covered by a bush.

Dr. Manford frowned.

"It looks like a miniature version of the needle-rock above us, sir."

"So it is!" Carl laughed. "Don't waste any more time in chatter. Get digging."

I planted the shovel blade first at the base of the miniature boulder, then stepped on it to push. *Thunk!*

I stopped and looked around. Everyone else had caught the significance of that.

The awed silence lasted several heartbeats. Then Dr. Manford said, "Let me have that."

He took the shovel and dug frantically.

Yes! Yes! Yes!

He quickly uncovered the top of a huge trunk.

He dropped to his knees and fumbled with an old lock. The clasp was so brittle with time, it pulled away from the trunk. Dr. Manford took a deep breath and slowly opened the lid.

We all gasped.

Sunshine poured and cascaded across a bounty of jewels and gold that filled the entire trunk.

"Millions," Doreen breathed. "Millions upon millions."

Dr. Manford jumped to his feet and threw his arms into the air. "We found it," he shouted at the top of his lungs. "We found it!"

"Yes," Carl said with a slight frown. "We found it."

"I'm sorry," Dr. Manford said sheepishly. "I just couldn't help myself." He stooped down again, and ran his fingers through the jewels.

There was a clattered of misplaced rocks behind us.

The first thing we saw was a long barrel of a rifle.

"What have we here?" a deep voice asked. The man behind the voice and the rifle was huge. Acne-scarred face, black turtleneck sweater, and unsmiling eyes.

Another man melted into view beside him. Slightly shorter, but wider. His shoulders dwarfed the straps from a backpack he carried. He had a cold, cold face with a flattened nose.

Dr. Manford stood and his eyes widened in panic.

Doreen spat. "You brutes. I hope you all rot in—"

Carl touched her shoulder. "Leave them, Doreen. They're not worth your hate."

"The kidnappers?" Lisa asked quietly. Ralphy nodded.

"Knock off the small talk. As you can see, we've got the weapons and the size. Now we want the treasure."

The shorter one stepped forward and hoisted his backpack down. He pulled from it two huge canvas duffel bags.

"This should do it," he grunted. "Start filling."

Carl stared steadily back at him.

The other man clicked the safety on the rifle and pointed it at Lisa. Carl squatted immediately and began throwing coins and jewels into the bag.

Dr. Manford was too stunned to help. The shorter man stepped forward and slapped him across the face. "You too. We don't feel like wasting time."

The clattering of the jewels and coins into the canvas bags became the only sounds.

Doreen then spoke quietly, "How long have you been following me?"

"Long enough, lady. And we appreciate your help."

Her eyes smoldered, but she made no other move except to pull Lisa in tight and place herself defiantly between Lisa and the rifle.

"Don't worry, lady. We only want the jewels."

I could not believe what I was seeing, but I saw no way out of the situation. About fifteen minutes later, Carl and Dr. Manford were finished.

Fifteen minutes, I told myself. *So much treasure that it took two grown men fifteen minutes to scoop it out.*

After the last jewel had clicked onto the top of the pile, there was only the sound of heavy breathing. Carl and Dr. Manford from exertion. The two men from greed.

"Much obliged, folks," the one with the rifle laughed. "We'll be on our way. Any of you try to follow before we get to the top of the cliffs, why I'll be forced to demonstrate how accurate this little rifle is."

Each of them grunted with the weight of their bags.

The tall one motioned to Lisa. "And just to be sure, I think we'll take you as hostage."

Lisa saw the evil in his eyes, and decided not to protest. She moved forward hesitantly. Carl tried to grab her arm, but a sudden movement of the rifle stopped him. "I can shoot her now, if you prefer," the man said with no emotion.

Carl stepped away.

The two men and Lisa reached the edge of the small plateau. No matter what, I had to stop them from taking Lisa.

I spoke as clearly as I could despite the blood pounding my temple.

"You might as well take Dr. Manford too," I said.

They spun around.

"Ricky!" Carl began.

The tall one cut him off with a wave of his hand. "Repeat that, kid."

When I spoke again, I felt more weary than afraid. "I said you might as well take Dr. Manford. After all, he's your boss."

23

Unfortunately, my accusation worked. Before anyone else could break the shocked silence, Dr. Manford moved ahead and joined the two men.

"Score one for the kid," he said through an icy smile. "What gave it away?"

I shrugged. "Just a lucky guess. The way you shouted 'I found it,' like it was a message to these two guys."

"Call it an unlucky guess, kid. You just bought yourself the last trouble you'll see in your life."

Maintaining his neutral voice, and watching us carefully, Dr. Manford then spoke to the shorter man. "Rope, dynamite, and timer."

He directed his voice at me again. "Now that all of you know who's behind this, you know too much to live." His smile became nasty. "Don't worry. We'll leave the girl with you."

Dr. Manford motioned to the shorter man, who had finished emptying his backpack. He roughly shoved Lisa back to where the rest of us waited.

The other man kept his rifle trained on us. His attention did not waver. He didn't give a split second for us to leap for escape.

The shorter one tied my hands first, looped the same rope around Lisa's hands, then, one at a time, around the others. He took a second length of rope, and did the same to our feet. With each tug of the rope, he grunted with effort to make the knots extra tight.

We might have had a chance, anyway, of untying each other, but the shorter thug then pushed us into a circle in the middle of the plateau. "Backs against each other," he snarled.

We did so. He slung more rope around us, and pulled so tight it took the air from my lungs.

"That should do it, boss. They could untie themselves, but not before the dynamite blows."

"Yes," Dr. Manford said, rubbing his chin thoughtfully. "And here I thought we would be using it for less exciting things, like excavating buried treasure. Oh well."

Dr. Manford squatted and began wiring a timer to a small bundle of dynamite. "We'll tie this nice little bundle to a rope, of course. Then tie that rope to, say, Ricky's leg. That way you won't be able to kick this stuff down the cliff."

It's not so strange that when very little of life appears to remain, it becomes so precious. I thought of Joel.

"Let my brother go, at least. He's too young to realize what's happening."

Dr. Manford's eyes became stone as he stared. Then he nodded. "We'll take him with us to the top of the cliffs. Someone will find him later, I'm sure."

The short thug untied Joel and retightened the rope.

Carl cleared his throat. "This is worth it? Killing three other children?"

Dr. Manford spun on him, and pointed at Doreen slumped by Carl. "That little old lady already gave up her life to search for the treasure. Ask her."

In the short silence that followed, the man with the rifle said, "Let's go before the sniveling starts."

"With our load, how long to reach the top of the cliffs?" Dr. Manford asked.

"Ten minutes," the short one replied.

"I'll set the timer for fifteen then."

"Make it half an hour," Carl said quietly.

Dr. Manford arched an eyebrow.

"We'll never get out of these ropes anyway," Carl said. "And it gives you longer to get away before anyone looks to see what caused the blast."

"What's your real reason?"

There was a pause.

"I want to pray," Carl said slowly. "Half an hour's not enough to make up for the last thirty years, but it's better than fifteen minutes."

"Twenty minutes is what you get."

Then he turned and walked away.

Joel tried staying.

"Go with them." I spoke around the lump in my throat at his loyalty. "We'll meet you at Carl's house for lunch."

I think Joel suspected different. He brought his teddy bear back and set it at my feet.

Then there was only the breeze tugging at the shrubs, the washing of waves on the sand far below us, and the light ticking of a timer on a bundle of dynamite at the end of a rope.

"I want to apologize," I started. Probably only a few minutes had passed. It seemed much longer.

"It's OK," Carl quickly said. "When I saw them leaving with Lisa, I was looking for a way to stall them too."

"Actually, sir, I wanted to apologize for lying. It wasn't a lucky guess. I just couldn't let Dr. Manford know that. Or things might be much worse right now."

Doreen sighed. "I'm afraid things can't get much worse. My hands are numb already. I'm guessing there's less than fifteen minutes left on the timer."

"We aren't without hope, ma'am. You see—"

"Ricky's right," Carl said with strength in his voice. "No matter what, we're never without hope. I've been a fool not to know that. I only wish it hadn't taken two days of kidnapping and a quarter-hour facing dynamite for me to realize it. I'd like us to pray together. To the God who I know is watching over us."

I grinned. It was a serious moment, but I thought maybe God too was smiling. There was something Carl didn't know. Something—because they were tied and all looking other directions—only I could see at that moment.

"Sir, could we hold off on that prayer?" I asked.

"I'd rather not." His voice came strongly over his shoulder. "We don't have much time left."

"More than you might guess, sir," I said, grinning wider, this time straight ahead.

Mike grinned back at me and wiggled his eyebrows mischievously.

"I hope you brought a knife with you, pal."

"Of course," he said. "I had to run back and get it. What do you think took me so long?"

* * * * * * * *

I will admit it was fun to keep them guessing by not explaining Mike's sudden miracle appearance. But I did have a better reason for my silence than mere fun.

The dynamite. A glance at the timer had shown sixteen minutes remaining when Mike began cutting. Twelve minutes had been left when he finished releasing us. Mike had been eager to throw the bundle of dynamite as far as he could toward the ocean. Carl, however, had warned against even touching the bundle, saying there was too much risk of accidentally triggering the timer. So we had scrambled and panted our way back up the rest of the cliffs and there had been zero opportunity to talk.

It wasn't until all of us had made it through the gate that led into Carl's backyard that the questions started.

"Mike, weren't you sick?" "How did you know where we were?" "How come you had a knife?"

Everybody was firing questions except for Carl. I noticed him back at the edge of the cliff. His head was bowed in silence.

And I sighed with relief. They had left Joel behind. He was waiting for us up ahead by the house.

Mike was shaking his head wildly. "I'll tell you later! We have to get the treasure back! I couldn't get the police here in time to be waiting for them and they could be miles away."

"You had time to call the police?" Ralphy asked.

"Why sure." Mike grinned broadly. "I was hiding in the pirate's tunnel the whole time. I saw everything from behind the secret door."

Doreen's jaw dropped. "You knew about the tunnel? How did

you happen to be there this morning anyway?"

"Yes, to the first question. Ricky's got the answer to the second question. And please, please no question number three. The treasure is getting away. We've got to get moving!"

I was just about to say something, when a shout from the side of the house interrupted us.

"Hey! What's this about Iranian rocket missiles and a spy ship?" The two cops ran forward, clutching their billy sticks. At this point, it didn't surprise me to be seeing Sam and Fred again.

"Iranian rocket missiles?" I hissed under my breath. "Mike, are you nuts?"

He shrugged. "It's all I could think of. You expect a dispatcher to believe the robbery of a hundred-year-old pirate's treasure?"

By that time, Sam was in front of us. He didn't look surprised, either. "I told you it was these whacko kids. I told the sergeant. I told the dispatcher. I told you, Fred. But no. All of you said we can't take the chance I was wrong. What if there's a spy ship parked down there, you all said. Well, look. Am I wrong? Nooooooooo. It's these whacko kids and another game."

"Your blood pressure, Sam."

"My friend did make up the story," I said. "But he had a great reason for it."

"Really?" Sam asked sarcastically. His face grew shiny red from frustration and anger.

"Yes, sir," Ralphy broke in excitedly and spoke quickly. "We just found a pirate's treasure. Two bags full. Millions and millions of dollars in jewels and old coins. Then some guys and a professor held us up at rifle point, roped us together, and tied a bundle full of dynamite to our rope."

Sam clenched his fists, lifted his chin to the sky, and yelled, "Aaaaarrgh!" He stopped, took a breath, and explained to his partner. "Doctor's orders, Fred. Stress release."

Doreen smiled a sweet old lady smile. "But officer. These boys are telling the truth."

"And the bandits are getting away!" Mike danced in nervousness to start pursuit.

"Lady, I'd like to believe you. But, after all, you do have a houseful of cats."

I held up a hand. Both cops were so weary, they didn't protest. "Did you pass a brown sedan in the middle of the road? Three guys in it?"

"They were out of gas, kid. Why? Did you siphon their gas?"

"No," I said. "I put ten pounds of sugar in the gas tank. If we leave now, we'll have no problem getting them. They won't leave without the treasure, and it's much too heavy to carry far."

Finally, Fred lost his temper. "That's it! You've just pushed us too far. I don't care what it takes, you're going to court on as many charges as I can lay. And—"

Carl was still at the edge of the cliff. He started walking toward us and waved a friendly wave at the cops.

Sam snorted. "Don't tell me you have this guy in on the story too. Maybe you're all loonies. The kidnapping was probably fake too. I mean really. A pirate's treasure. Dynamite? Wait till the judge hears—"

He didn't finish his sentence.

WHOOOOOOOOMMMMMMMMMP!

The bundle blew, sending a fireball that towered briefly above the cliffs. The ground shook underneath us. Almost immediately, there was a clattering of rocks tumbling down the cliff. And shortly after, a high dust cloud that began dispersing in the ocean breeze.

Both cops looked at each other. Sam shook his head sadly.

Fred opened his mouth once, twice, like a guppy in a fish tank. Finally the words came out. "Sam, I think I need therapy."

25

"Weird things happening around here," Mike commented.

"Yup," I said. "Just when you get used to a cat lady, she decides to become normal. How weird."

Ralphy squinted across the lawn. "That's the third SPCA van! She must be getting rid of them all. What possible reason would she have for that?"

Lisa tossed her hair. "Men," she said. "You wouldn't know a hammer if it hit you between the eyes."

Mike, Ralphy, and I looked at each other. "Huh?" we all said at once.

"I think it's sweet and if you guys can't figure it out, then I'm certainly not telling."

That's real logic, I told myself. But I didn't concern myself too much wondering. It was too much fun watching grown men chase cats.

It was mid-afternoon, barely hours after the police had arrested Dr. Manford and his two thugs as they hobbled down the street trying to carry the heavy canvas bags filled with treasure. Although so little time had passed, already I was having a hard time believing everything that had happened. To make it more confusing, Doreen was shipping her cats out.

We watched Hezekiah and Joel saying goodbye on the lawn, and an SPCA man coming toward them. Hezekiah swiped and ran away.

"Good afternoon," came Carl's voice from behind us. "Doreen

has sandwiches ready in the kitchen for all of us."

Back inside Carl's house, Lisa noticed it first. "Uncle Carl! No ponytail!"

Mike, quick as ever, said, "No goatee!"

Carl merely smiled. "That's right." He looked at me. "OK, this morning you made me a deal. You'd tell me about the behind-the-scenes work with Mike, if I'd tell you about the bag of money."

"Yes, sir."

"I'm ready."

"So am I," I said. I began waiting. So did Carl.

Ralphy groaned. He reached into his pocket and flipped a coin onto the kitchen table. "Heads. You go first, Ricky."

I was conscious of everybody's eyes on me. Until now, the excitement of the treasure and the arrival of the SPCA vans had given no opportunity to explain. Not even Mike knew the full story.

"When did I start suspecting the fake Dr. Manford? A ladybug told me."

This time, it was Mike who groaned.

"Honest," I insisted. I told them about the ladybug stuck on the book cover in the library. "I should have wondered why the cover was sticky. The reason, of course, was because someone had just pulled the book jacket off. You know, libraries always tape book jackets onto the cover. With the jacket gone, the recent tape marks were still sticky."

"Well that makes sense," Mike said sarcastically.

"It does if you start thinking about book jackets. They usually have the author's picture on the back. Who wouldn't want people to see that picture? Why not? And who knew I was going to the library that morning in the first place?"

Mike nodded thoughtfully. "Dr. Manford. I remember now. He made up an excuse for you to go to the beach. That gave him time to beat you to the library."

"Exactly. Once I began to doubt that he was the real Dr. Manford, a few other things made sense. Like the tiny cardboard cards I saw in the garbage."

Carl shook his head. "That'll need explaining too."

"There were handfuls of them, sir. It bugged me, not knowing what they were, or from where. Yesterday, when the fake Dr. Manford pulled a brand-new handkerchief from his pocket, I knew. Handkerchiefs—new in packages—are wrapped around those stiff cardboards. Who and why would anyone need so many new handkerchiefs? The fake Dr. Manford, of course, because of his allergy to cats. Why? Because he was in contact with people who were regularly in Doreen's house—the kidnappers. That too explained the flashing Ralphy once saw from the third-story window of Doreen's house. They were probably signaling to the fake Dr. Manford in the third story of Carl's house."

I continued in a rush. "Then the rest made sense. Dr. Manford might have called the police to investigate the kidnapping, but he could also warn the kidnappers in Doreen's house."

I turned to Doreen. "I'm sure they sent you down the stairs and threatened to hurt Ralphy and Joel if you let the police inside. Did the phone ring a few minutes before?"

She nodded.

"However," I said, "I wanted to be quite certain before I put sugar in his gas tank. Last night, I snuck out of the house to a pay phone. It cost me most of Mike's pocket change, but I called Information in Dallas and got Dr. Manford's home number. Texas is two hours behind so I didn't think it was too late in the evening to call him. That's when I found out he has been in the hospital for the last few months."

"What!" Carl exclaimed. "But I had letters from him. I never heard about a hospital stay."

"Car accident, sir. Dr. Manford's personal secretary kept a correspondence going with you, as if Dr. Manford himself was writing. Guess why."

Carl spoke slowly as it dawned on him. "Because his personal secretary decided it was the ideal time to come out here and impersonate Dr. Manford."

"That's right, sir. The fake Dr. Manford. Some of Dr. Manford's recent research indicated the treasure was very close by the house. The personal secretary saw it as the perfect chance to look for himself. He could leave with the treasure, and by the time anyone figured out who he was, he would be long gone."

Carl leaned back and whistled a low tuneless whistle. "So, knowing all this, you had Mike watch from the tunnel while the rest of us searched for treasure."

Mike grinned. "It was great. We thought it was the best way to smoke out the kidnappers and prove without a doubt who was really behind all of this. But it nearly killed me. I ran once to the house to call the cops. Then I ran down in time to see them tie you up. So I had to run back up to the house to get a knife, and run back down in time to cut you free."

"Good thing," Ralphy said. "But I would have been less scared if Ricky had let us in on this beforehand."

"I was worried one of us might give it away before the fake Dr. Manford revealed himself."

"Thanks, pal."

I was finished speaking. Yet Carl was in no hurry to let us know about the paper bag of money.

Instead, he closed his eyes and said, "Let me tell you about my ponytail."

Epilogue

Before he could say another word, Joel wandered into the kitchen. I flipped him his teddy bear.

Carl smiled at that. He then closed his eyes again. "In the '60s, I was what they called a hippie. We were into being rebels, making the world a better place, growing our hair long, and, unfortunately, doing drugs. I lived in San Francisco. I also fell in love and married. That was strange; hippies didn't really believe in marriage. But this love was the absolute real thing and I rebelled by getting married. That's funny, right? Rebelling against the rebels.

"I believed in God back then. The whole world was cool, I was in love, and God was in charge of the cosmos. Who could ask for more? Better yet, my love, my sweet, sweet love, was going to have a baby."

Carl's face darkened as he struggled with memories. "The baby was two weeks earlier than the doctors predicted. That's normally not a problem, but I was so wrecked on drugs that night, I didn't know what was happening."

A slight groan escaped him. His eyes were still closed. "They died. I should have gotten them to the hospital in time. But I was too wrecked. The details—I don't want to think about the details—are not important. When I came down from that drug-induced high, they were both gone. My sweet love, and the child that was to be ours."

The kitchen was absolutely still. Carl's pain filled all of us.

"I wanted to die myself. Instead, I decided to punish myself by living, and remembering. I vowed to keep my ponytail. I did not want a single day to pass without looking in the mirror and seeing it as a reminder of that night."

Joel moved next to me and pressed against my leg. He too felt the pain.

Carl's voice grew softer. "The ponytail was also a reminder to me that I would deny God. Although I was responsible for their deaths, I wanted to blame Him, so I chose not to believe."

He opened his eyes and looked around the kitchen. "Nearly thirty years I lived like that. Thirty years of seeing this ponytail in the mirror. Until this weekend.

"Locked in that room, tied to a chair, and not knowing whether I would live or die, broke a dam inside me. Then, through the bedroom wall, hearing Ralphy and Joel pray with a simple faith started me back to God. And facing death on the cliff this morning suddenly made me glad that I had had enough time to get back to God in my heart."

He opened his hands at his sides and shrugged with a smile. "So I chopped off the ponytail. It was time to live again, and to believe."

There was a respectful quiet for a few minutes.

"But sir," Mike finally spoke. "That doesn't explain the bag of money, or Big Joe, or a midnight meeting in front of the house last week."

Carl grinned. "Actually, it does. You were almost right with your drugs theory. Except I was fighting drugs."

"Fighting drugs," Lisa repeated.

Carl nodded. "It wasn't anything I really wanted to tell you, because I didn't feel ready to explain about the ponytail. The money is my way of trying to make up for what happened on that terrible night. Big Joe knows the street people. I trust him to give cash to those who need it most, whether they're drug addicts or children of drug addicts. He stopped by that night with a gift from a mother whose son Big Joe had helped through a bad week.

"Big Joe knew I was in danger, because I missed a Saturday meeting with him and had not called to tell him why. That was too unusual to mean anything good. But he couldn't say much to Lisa, because the only condition I made with him was that he never tell anyone about the money."

Carl noticed how Lisa's eyes shone with adoration.

"The money's not a big deal," he protested to her. "Writing screenplays has brought me more money than I can ever spend. Without a family to care for..."

Then he grinned. "... at least until now."

Lisa giggled. But I still didn't understand.

Lisa caught the look on my face. "Ricky, you chowderhead. Are you blind? Why do you think Doreen is moving the cats out?"

I laughed, remembering suddenly how Doreen and Carl had been spending so much time together, whispering and holding hands, how Doreen's face looked so much younger this morning, and how I had mistakenly thought it was the excitement of the treasure hunt. "True love?" I squeaked. "But they're, they're..."

Doreen finished for me with a giggle of her own. "Too old?"

I nodded with a red face.

"We both thought so, too. But spending two days together with nothing to do but talk, and, well..." Doreen's face flushed a little, as she struggled to complete the sentence.

Ralphy let her off the hook. "Bummer about the treasure."

Carl and Doreen shrugged. Doreen said, "After the government officials get through with deciding who really owns it, and after they decide how much to tax, it will take years before we see any money. Some will go to your college funds, some to drug rehab programs. The treasure just isn't important to me anymore."

She smiled shyly and squeezed Carl's hand.

"Hey!" Mike said as a thought struck him. "Carl, why is your goatee gone?"

Carl began stuttering. He looked at Doreen for help, but she only smiled and turned redder.

That's when Joel moved away from my leg.

He stepped into the middle of the kitchen, away from all of us, and with a flourish, brought his teddy bear into both arms.

He leaned forward, and pulled the teddy bear close to his face. Then *began kissing it?*

Before anyone could react, he pushed the teddy bear away from him.

With a voice raised to sound uncannily like Doreen's, he spoke sweetly to the teddy bear, "Oh Bubsy-wuds, I do enjoy a good smooch. But it would be sooo much better if your chin were smooth."

"Bubsy-wuds?" Mike and Ralphy and I echoed at the same time.

"Aaaaaack! How did that squirt ever . . ." Carl left the table with hands outstretched and feet running.

But he didn't have a chance. Joel was out the door and gone before Carl had taken two steps.

Disappearing, after all, comes natural to Joel.

SIGMUND BROUWER was born in 1959 to Dutch immigrant parents in Red Deer, Alberta, Canada. For many years after high school graduation he seemed incapable of holding a steady job, despite (or because of) two separate university degrees.

From slaughterhouse butchering to heavy-duty truck driving to semi-pro hockey, he ardently pursued any type of work that did not lead to becoming a lawyer, his mother's fondest dream.

After years of traveling, to the relief of his warm and loving Christian family, he returned home and has since donned a cloak of respectability as a former senior editor of *National Racquetball*, an international magazine published from Florida, as a current publisher of various local weekly magazines, and as writing instructor at the local college.

He now spends much of his writing time in conference with Ricky and Joel Kidd. Many of the resulting short stories with them and the rest of the Accidental Detectives have appeared in various magazines in the United States, Canada, and Australia.

Sigmund has no intention of leaving his hometown again, except, of course, to travel.

Next in the Accidental Detectives...

Ahead, breaking through the mists, was the serpentine neck and head matching exactly the illustrations given for the Ogopogo lake monster.

"It can't be!" Ralphy hissed as he cocked his head to listen below. "I don't hear any frantic beeping."

"It's on the surface," I whispered back. "The scanner must be missing it completely."

The boat glided forward. Mists swirled. Captain Luke, I'm sure, had not seen it yet.

Ralphy strained to see it better. The mist seemed to drape the figure. One moment, there. The next, not.

I felt Ralphy brush against me as he strained harder to look.... The boat lurched, and Ralphy toppled overboard into the icy mountain lake water and disappeared.

For too many heartstopping moments, none of us reacted. Ralphy was in water deeper than we could imagine with the suddenly real possibility of a lake monster able to pull him down forever!

Captain Luke came whipping around the side of the deck. "I'll get him!" he shouted as he scrambled to get out of his heavy jacket. His franticness, however, caused him to slip, and he banged his head against the deck, then groaned once before passing out completely.

Ralphy appeared briefly on the surface! "G . . . get me," he sputtered weakly. "Before a monster does!"

. . . in CREATURE OF THE MISTS